THE MILLION DOLLAR RACE

Also by Matthew Ross Smith

Lizzy Legend

THE MILLION DOLLAR RACE

MATTHEW ROSS SMITH

ALADDIN
New York London Toronto Sydney New Delhi

ALADDIN

An imprint of Simon & Schuster Children's Publishing Division

1230 Avenue of the Americas, New York, New York 10020

First Aladdin hardcover edition January 2021

Text © 2021 by Matthew Ross Smith

Jacket illustration © 2021 by Oriol Vidal

All rights reserved, including the right of reproduction in whole or in part in any form.

ALADDIN and related logo are registered trademarks of Simon & Schuster, Inc.

For information about special discounts for bulk purchases, please contact Simon & Schuster Special Sales at 1-866-506-1949 or business@simonandschuster.com.

The Simon & Schuster Speakers Bureau can bring authors to your live event. For more information or to book an event contact the Simon & Schuster Speakers Bureau at 1-866-248-3049 or visit our website at www.simonspeakers.com.

Book designed by Heather Palisi

The text of this book was set in Legacy.

Manufactured in the United States of America 1220 FFG

2 4 6 8 10 9 7 5 3 1

Library of Congress Cataloging-in-Publication Data

Names: Smith, Matthew Ross, author.

Title: The million dollar race / by Matthew Ross Smith.

Description: First Aladdin hardcover edition. | New York : Aladdin, 2021. | Audience: Ages 8-12. | Summary: "When Grant Falloon's dreams of winning the Babblemoney Games are hindered by his parents' alternative lifestyle, he creates his own internet country to get back into the competition"— Provided by publisher.

Identifiers: LCCN 2020023133 (print) | LCCN 2020023134 (ebook) | ISBN 9781534420274 (hardcover) | ISBN 9781534420298 (ebook)

Subjects: CYAC: Contests—Fiction. | Family life—Fiction. | Eccentrics and eccentricities—Fiction. | Best friends—Fiction. | Friendship—Fiction.

Classification: LCC PZ7.1.S6447 Mil 2021 (print) | LCC PZ7.1.S6447 (ebook) | DDC [Fic]—dc23

LC record available at https://lccn.loc.gov/2020023133

LC ebook record available at https://lccn.loc.gov/2020023134

For Georgia

THE MILLION DOLLAR RACE

Once in every lifetime, they say, if everything goes just right—if you eat just the right combination of foods, if you get just the right amount of sleep, if you've worked hard and given absolutely *everything* of yourself—it can happen. You can do it. You can close your hand around the dream you've been chasing your whole life.

You can catch the lightning.

It's not just a myth. I've *seen* it. I watched in 2009 as Usain Bolt set the 100-meter world record—9.58 seconds. Granted, I was only a baby, plopped in front of the TV. But I like to think experiences, even if we don't remember them, leave little seeds in us.

For years I've been nurturing this seed, shaping the weather of my life so that, under the brightest lights, it'll activate and burst up through the soil.

Today feels like the day.

I, Grant Falloon, am about to make history.

It's the Penn Relays. Biggest track meet of the year. The bleachers are packed beneath the triangular flags atop Franklin Field. I'm in lane four. I shake my legs. Roll my neck. On the announcer's cue, I kneel and press my spikes into the blocks.

"Runners on your marks."

I close my eyes. My mind is a glowing computer screen. One by one I drag the cluttered files into the trash. Everything must go. Thoughts are heavy. I need to be light. I need to be *fast*. The boys' record (U-13) is 10.73 seconds.

"Runners set."

My head drops. My hips lift.

Beep!

I explode out of the blocks, head down.

I drive my legs. Elbows in. Fingers fully extended.

It's happening. I feel myself pulling ahead. Not only ahead of the pack but also—this is hard to explain—of *myself*. Reaching top speed, I feel myself edging out of the me-shaped outline I was born into.

Just a half step.

And it's the best feeling in the world.

I'm feeling so invincible that, twenty meters from the

line, I forget the number one rule of sprinting. KEEP. YOUR. EYES. ON. THE. PRIZE.

I peek into the crowd. My family's in section 102. There's Mom: fierce, wild-eyed, yelling, "Goooooo!" Dad's peeking between his fingers like he's watching a horror movie. Franny's holding his phone up, filming.

That's all it takes. A fraction of a second. A *glance*. And my toe catches. It's like I've tripped on an invisible root. Suddenly I'm stumbling. Flailing. Arms wheeling.

And yet . . .

I'm so close!

I spill forward, arms extended Superman style. The finish line is flying toward me. All I have to do is wait, and it's going to cross me.

But then gravity.

My chest hits first. I bounce. My hips crash down. My legs fly up. My chin scrapes along the track one, two, three times.

I skid, arms outstretched.

Reaching desperately.

But no.

No.

I lie facedown on the track, a literal inch from the finish line. It's eerily silent, probably because all ten thousand people have their hands over their mouths.

I can't look. If I look, then it's real. What if I just lie here for a while? What if I just lie here till the stadium

3

empties? Then I can tiptoe home and put a Band-Aid on my bleeding chin, and it'll be like nothing happened.

Right?

Or, just to be safe, I'll lie here till school lets out and everyone forgets. I'll lie here till the birds fly south, till the autumn leaves twirl down on top of me.

I'll lie here till the whole human race dies out and the grass pushes up through the track and the squirrels build a new civilization in the ruins.

Six weeks have passed since my epic spill at the Penn Relays. The video—posted by my brother—now has 8.4 million views. In slow motion you can actually see me mouthing *Noooooooooooooo* as I go down.

Within hours, people edited the video so I was tumbling into the Grand Canyon, a wormhole in space, etc.

The meme became such a sensation that the producers of *The Midnight Show! with Jaime Freeman* even invited me to New York to joke about it.

I said thanks, but no thanks.

Last thing I need is for *more* people to see what happened . . .

I'm over at Jay's house now. That's my best friend and number one rival. He was in second place when I tripped. He would've won if he hadn't stopped to peel me off the track. He didn't *mean* to stop, he said, almost apologizing. He just *did*.

We crossed the line together, tying for dead-last place.

His mom got an aboveground pool last week so she can do her exercises, her "pool-lates," as she calls them (cracks herself up every time). I'm draped over a bright pink pool noodle, floating in slow, hypnotic circles. I have no idea what day of the week it is, or what time. It's summer break. Sometime between meals.

"You see the one of the ape with the cell phone?" Jay says, using his finger to sign his autograph on the surface of the water.

"Remind me," I say.

"So you see this ape. Someone gives him an iPhone to see what he'll do. He holds it up, squinting like, *What's this? Is it food?* He sniffs it. Then, swear to god, he just sits down and starts taking all these selfies. They couldn't get it away from him."

"That's awesome. What'd they do?"

"Nothin'. They couldn't get it back. Finally he just typed a bunch of poop emojis and chucked it against the wall."

I dunk myself in the water and wipe my face with a quick downward swipe. The sunglasses on top of Jay's head are his newest accessory. If you visualized us as video game characters, spinning in the character select screen, his Style and Coolness would be maxed out. My Speed would be slightly higher, but everything else would be super low.

"I was thinkin'," he says, reaching for his store-brand soda on the edge of the pool. "We should do a little project this summer, like the old days."

"What? Like gluing buttons onto construction paper?"

"Nah. Let's take it up a level."

"Popsicle sticks?"

"We should make a reality TV show."

"Ha. About what?"

"Your family."

"Stop."

"I'm serious!" he says. "I'll film it on my phone. We can set up a confessional in the garage, and you'll be like, *And then I got a four-pound organic carrot in my Easter basket!* People will eat that mess up. We'll be so rich."

When we talk about getting rich—our favorite topic—it's always *we*, something *we'll* do together, our destinies joined like the lanes of a track meeting at the horizon.

"What's a confessional?" I say.

"It's, like, where you talk directly to the camera and spill your guts and say lots of backstabby stuff."

I lie back and float on the foam noodle. High above, a plane draws a white line on the sky. "Cool," I say. "We'll have to blur my face, though. I've had enough infamy for one lifetime."

Infamy, the way I understand it, is when you're famous for the *wrong* reasons.

Like, say, falling on your face in the biggest race of your life.

Jay leans back, frowning. "You're still sweatin' that?"

Before I can answer, his mom comes out. She's in a one-piece bathing suit and a bathing cap. "Out," she says, swatting the air. "You slobs are messin' up my pool."

"It's not a pool," Jay says. "It's an oversized dunk tank."

"Out!"

3

Mrs. Fa'atasi—Jay's mom—is obsessed with seashells. Last summer, when she and Jay visited family in Samoa, she brought back a whole suitcase full. She keeps them on a bookshelf in the living room. She says that, if you listen close, each one whispers a different story. I try to listen sometimes, but I only hear my own echoing thoughts.

Coming in from the backyard, I open a fresh box of parmesan Cheez-Its without asking (see Rights of a Best Friend, subsection 9, clause 4), and we sit at the kitchen table in our dripping-wet bathing suits. A picture of Jay's older brother glints on the fridge. He's in his Marine blues, holding a sword. "You hear from Tua?" I ask.

"Nah."

"Everything cool?"

"Yeah. Said he'd call again in a few weeks."

"You think that means some crazy-secret mission?"

Jay shrugs. I wish I hadn't brought it up.

"So about our show," he says, reaching across the table for the Cheez-Its. "I'm thinkin' we'll call it *Last Family on Earth*."

I laugh. *"Why?"*

"That's how we'll pitch it. Like you, the wacky Falloons, are the last family on earth. We'll follow you around and see what you do."

"What about, like, all the other people in the world? Won't they ruin the premise? Walking around in the background and stuff?"

"We can edit them out in post."

"I thought you said this was a *reality* show."

"It is."

"I don't think you understand what a reality show is," I say.

"I don't think *you* understand what a reality show is."

Fair point since my family doesn't own a TV. But I watch plenty of it here. Since the summer began, I've spent way more time at Jay's house than my own. Sometimes I pretend that Mrs. Fa'atasi has adopted me and Jay is my brother for real.

"So what's the deal?" Jay says. "Can we do it? The show?"

"Sorry," I say, lacing my fingers behind my head like a fat-cat TV executive. "It's just not for me. But I wish you the best of luck, kid."

Jay leans forward, studying me. "Can I tell you something about yourself, bro? For real? It's like you were born in a gold mine—"

"Ha. Right."

"A *gold* mine, but the little light on your helmet doesn't work. Your family is *hilarious*. You just can't see it. You're too close."

I squirm. The cold air-conditioning is clinging to my wet skin.

"I'm not making fun of you," he says. "I'm saying your family is weird and awesome and you can't see it. Can we please just film one episode? Please?"

"I'm sorry," I say. "I do not consent."

4

My family doesn't own a car. We used to, but last year Mom sold it and bought us all new street bikes and matching helmets. That's why we're riding to the Food Palace in our usual "peloton"—a single-file line of bikes. It's how we get everywhere.

"Pothole!" Mom yells. "Incoming!"

I regrip my handlebars and swerve around the puddle-filled crater. Ahead in the bike lane, Mom, Dad, and Franny pump their legs in unison, orange construction vests glinting in the morning sun. "Let's go!" Franny yells, peeking back. "Push it!"

Soaring downhill, our bikes sound like unspooling fishing lines. *Zzzzzz.*

We glide around a moving van with its flashers on. A mail truck. A street sweeper. There's a heavy, satisfying clunk as I stand on my pedals and switch gears. Back uphill now. Row houses on both sides, pressed beneath the summer sky.

My helmet is tightly buckled beneath my chin. I smear my forearm across my sweaty face. Sunscreen burns in my—

"Red light!"

I skid to a stop. Soles down.

"You okay?" Dad asks.

"I'm fine," I say, blinking hard.

"You—"

"I'm *fine*."

As we lock up in the parking lot, my little brother—only a year younger than me—unclips his helmet. He shakes out his shoulder-length black hair and says, "Good ride, team!" He tries to give me a high five, but I just shake my head.

"Remind me to get the stuff for the shrimp," Mom says, reknotting her bandanna.

"It's not shrimp," I say. "It's tofu that you cut into shrimplike shapes."

"I think it's de-li-cious," Franny says, rubbing his belly. He waits till Mom and Dad look away . . . then makes a devil face and sticks his tongue out at me.

Inside the grocery store, I linger in front of the produce section, eyes closed, letting the cool mist soak my hot face. Some families go to church on Sunday mornings. I have this.

"Come on," Dad says. "I need help with the yogurt."

He has a special deal with the manager. We get all their just-expired yogurt for half off. An expiration date, Dad says, is "just an arbitrary line drawn for legal reasons."

Which is true, I guess. Most just-expired food is still perfectly edible and would end up in a landfill if we didn't eat it. Mom jokes Dad's gravestone will say:

DAVE FALLOON

1986–20XX

LET'S JUST GET THE CHEAPER ONE

A little girl's in the checkout lane beside us. Pigtails. Sippy cup. Legs dangling from the shopping cart.

Her eyes widen, taking us in: Dad in his purple velvet coat and his thick, bristly mustache. Mom—the public defender—aka the Lawyer You Get If You Can't Afford a Lawyer—in her paint-splattered overalls from Second Time Around. Franny—the YouTube star—smoothing his thick eyebrows, mugging into his phone camera.

And *me*, of course, the gangly, freckle-faced track star in mesh shorts, standing as far from them as I can physically get, hunched like a lowercase *r*.

It's true: I stare at the floor so much it's actually wrecked my posture.

"*Thanks!*" Dad says to the checkout lady. "*Have a fantastic day!*"

Biking home—laden with heavy bags—I can't stop thinking about that little girl in the checkout aisle. Crazy as it sounds . . . I can still feel it.

Her stare.

It's just like when I walk down the hall at school. I could take a weeklong bath in bleach, and they'd still be there—*the stares.*

No amount of scrubbing can wash them off.

It's part of why I love running so much. Why I'm so addicted to the racing life. If I'm moving fast enough, people can't really see me.

The stares don't stick.

5

When we get back from the Food Palace, I have a text from Jay:

J: yooooooooo u hear??????

              G: am i where

J: not here
J: smh
J: HEAR

              G: oh
              G: shut up

J: (typing . . .)

G: if i recall
G: UR the one who failed english . . .

J: not true
J: i failed that ONE book report . . .

G: lol
G: u told mr johnson books are just "really long twitter threads u scroll sideways instead of down"

J: i stand by that!!!

G: lol
G: did I HEAR what?

J: check it!!
J: [web link]

Youth Competition Announced
Rock View, CA—Kids around the world are invited to compete in what's being called the Million Dollar Race. The winners—one boy and one girl, aged 11–13—will receive a trust fund worth one

million dollars and a lifetime sponsorship deal from the Babblemoney Sneaker Company.

"As I'm getting older, I've been thinking a lot about my own childhood, and how it shaped my whole life," said Esther Babblemoney, the so-called Sneaker Queen worth over $50 billion. "I want to inspire the next generation of champions to chase their dreams and not let anything or anyone stand in their way."

Local qualifiers will be held on July 7. National qualifiers on July 27. The finals will be August 12 at the famed Babblemoney Estate in California.

G: ahhhhhhhh!!!!!
G: bro this is amazing!!!!
G: im literally jumping on my bed

J: i know!!!!!
J: it's awesome
J: everyone's talking about it

G: (typing . . .)

J: i hate to even ask . . .
J: but uh . . .
J: ur parents gonna let u sign up???

6

When I have to explain our Family Council to people, I say, *Imagine our family as its own, very tiny country.*

THE REPUBLIC OF FALLOON, POPULATION: 4. We're a self-governing democracy. Any decision affecting the family must be approved by a majority vote of its citizens.

That's why I've called everyone here to the living room. This current "ballot measure" (thing we're voting on) is pretty minor—I need Mom and Dad's permission to register for the Million Dollar Race.

As with any government, there are backroom dealings and secret alliances. The most powerful group is the Anti-Dad Caucus. At least once per week me, Mom, and Franny have to shoot down one of his harebrained ideas.

Most recently he proposed we sell our house, move to El Salvador, and become bean farmers.

The three of them are on the lime-green couch we've had for as long as I can remember. Dad's in the middle, in his "workout clothes," a spindly white tank top and thigh-revealing bike shorts that, with his mustache, make him look like one of those old-timey boxers that say "put up your dukes."

Mom's still in her wrinkled lawyer suit, sipping an extra-fizzy club soda. We have one of those carbonate-your-own-water machines, and she's obsessed. I hear it *tssssting* through the night.

Franny's slouched in the corner, making fish lips at his phone camera.

Getting our phones was the only legislation me and Franny have ever cosponsored. Neither of us liked working together, but being trapped in this house without a connection to the outside world was becoming suffocating.

We had to get it done.

Right when I'm about to start talking, Franny pans the camera across the three of us, gathering raw footage for his next vlog. His YouTube channel, *The Franny Files*, has 350,000 subscribers. He releases a new episode every Friday, each more ridiculous than the last. Last week it was just a montage of all his burps from the week. At the end he layered them together like a symphony.

Technically Mom and Dad own the account, since

he's only twelve, but he's got this whole plan that when he turns eighteen, he'll immediately monetize the account and become an overnight millionaire.

To be honest, I think that's part of the reason I'm so excited about this race. Winning that trust fund would make me—the older brother—top dog again, restoring the natural order of things. I already know what I'd do with the dough. I'd buy a mansion on a private island, surrounded by a twenty-foot-high gate. I'd put a giant flat-screen TV on every wall, in every room. Jay would come over and we'd train all morning on my state-of-the-art track and then we'd float around in my sneaker-shaped pool.

"As our first order of business," I say, pacing the living room in my white socks and slip-on sandals, "I motion that Franny stop recording this."

"Nay!" Franny says, turning his phone around to grin at the camera.

I cross my arms. *"Mom."*

Yes, we're a democracy. Yes, every vote counts. But here's the thing. Beneath all the pomp and ceremony, everyone knows Mom's really in charge. She's like the Speaker of the Living Room. If you need something, you can appeal directly to her.

"All who support Franny putting his phone away, say aye," she says.

"Aye!" I say.

"Aye," Dad says.

Franny makes fish lips to the camera again, ignoring us.

Mom's neck is her anger indicator. It's like an alert in a nuclear power plant—if it's flashing red, you know you're in serious trouble.

"*Francis,*" she says, hands still folded tightly in her lap. "If you don't turn that phone off right now, you're not going to see it for a month."

Technically this would take a motion to approve.

But . . . you know.

7

"Fine," Franny says. He slides the phone onto the coffee table and sits back petulantly.

"So," I say, glaring at him, "as I was *trying* to say, there's this new race sponsored by the Babblemoney Company. The winner gets a million bucks and a lifetime sponsorship deal. I need your permission to sign up."

Any other family, the conversation is over.

Great! Wow! Good luck, son!

With us?

Get comfortable. This could take a while. . . .

Our family motto is "Skepsis!" which is an ancient Greek word that means, basically, "question everything." It's where we get the English word "skeptical."

"Now let's think about this," Dad says, tapping his finger on his bottom lip. "Why would they—a huge shoe company—do such a thing?"

"Because it's fun," I say.

"Mmm. In my experience 'fun' is not often the motivation of ruthless multinational corporations. I'm sure there were *many* meetings about this at the highest levels."

"The old lady who runs it doesn't know what to do with all her money," I explain. "She wants to give back before she dies."

This wins me a few nods.

My family is big into "giving back."

"I'm getting some strong *Charlie and the Chocolate Factory* vibes here," Mom says, picking a fuzzy off the couch. "And we all remember how *that* ended."

"Um, with Charlie inheriting the company and becoming an overnight bazillionaire?"

"Is that how it ended? I thought it was darker. . . ."

"Dahl was a fairly capable satirist," Dad says, lifting one of his skinny legs and placing it over the other. "In fact, if you look at some of his adult work—"

"They're right," Franny says. "This whole thing stinks like a dead fish."

I can't believe this. All I need is a freaking signature on a permission form. *I should've just forged it.*

"Let me ask you this," Mom says. "I think I know why *they're* having the competition. But why do *you* want to be a part of it?"

"Do you even have to ask?" I say.

"I want to hear it in your own words."

"Because it's awesome. It's on ESPN. The winner gets a truckload of cash. Lifetime sponsorship. And—"

"And *what*?"

I look over at the blown-up photo of us on the dining room wall. We're in Sea Isle, five years ago, all of us wearing matching tie-dye shirts. Seeing us all so happy like that, sticking our tongues out, makes me crushingly sad. I want to get a pair of scissors and cut myself out of the picture. It'd be so much easier to hate my family if I didn't have to remember—if I didn't know, deep down—that I love them.

"You guys don't get it," I say. "Everyone in the world thinks I'm just some goof who fell on his face in the biggest race of his life. I mean, I *am*, it happened . . . but what I'm saying is . . . that's not the real me. I can *win* this thing. I know I can. And if I don't take this chance now, if I can't even *try*, I'll regret it for the rest of my life. Please don't take this away from me. *Please*."

It's considered poor form to beg at the Family Council.

But whatever.

I'm just keeping it real.

Mom's got a sensor in her ear that reads the sincerity of human voices. It's why she's such a good lawyer. "Okay," she says. "I vote yes."

Dad leans back and sucks in a deep breath like he's really agonizing. "Okay. I guess I don't see the harm. . . ."

Franny doesn't matter anymore, but he still gets to vote, family rules.

"*Aye*," he says. "But my objections are noted. I still think this thing *stinks*. I don't know how or why. But I'm gonna get to the bottom of it."

The council adjourns. I race up the steps, two at a time, and do a victory lap around my bedroom. I skim my fingertips across the double waterfall of prize ribbons and gold medals hanging above my desk—so many that I had to hammer in a second nail last year to hold more, and both nails are tilted down from the weight.

8

"Come on!" I yell the next morning. "Power through! Last one!"

Me and Jay are training together at the middle school track. It's our standard workout, a mix of leg raises, side sweeps, reverse crunches, side planks, kettle bells, and box jumps—everything designed to make us more explosive.

Sometimes I complain about training because everyone else does, but, if I'm being honest...

I love it.

I love the feeling of my lungs expanding in my chest on a cool summer morning. I love it when the ball of my foot strikes at just the right angle, my calf muscles engaging, my quads, my hips, my core, all in perfect rhythm.

It's only when I'm running that I feel the clutter of my thoughts thinning, something pure and bright shining underneath.

As we push through our last set, I visualize myself breaking the world record. In my mind, I flex for the cameras like Usain Bolt and look up into a blizzard of golden confetti. From the glint in Jay's eye, I can tell he's imagining the same thing.

After training we stop for lunch at Frank's Pizza. The smell of mozzarella sticks is intoxicating, but, with the big race coming up, I order a salad with grilled chicken.

"So listen," I say, sliding an oregano shaker between my hands. "Let's be real. We both wanna win this thing."

Jay flicks a quarter and follows its path across the red-topped table with his finger. "*Obviously,*" he says. "What's your point?"

"I just don't want this to wreck our friendship."

"Why would it wreck our friendship?"

"Because if one of us qualifies at regionals. That means . . ."

He stops the quarter beneath his finger. Unlike mine, his fingernails are neatly clipped. "It's all good, bro. Same as always. No mercy, no hard feelings. Cool?"

"Cool," I say.

We fist-bump.

The owner of the pizza shop brings out our food. He's been wearing the same greasy apron since 1979.

The flour on his face makes him look like a sweaty, gold-chain-wearing ghost. "You two bums ever gonna pay me or what?"

"We *told* you," Jay says, "you're *sponsoring* us. Remember?"

"Oh yeah. Right. And what do *I* get outta that?"

"When we're rich and famous," I say, "we'll tell everyone that we never coulda done it without Frank's Pizza, home of the famous Upside Down!"

We both give a double thumbs-up, smiling with extra cheese.

Frank punches numbers into an imaginary calculator in his palm. "Nah," he says. "Still won't cover it."

9

After what feels like an endless chain of days, the morning of the regional qualifier finally arrives. *"Chew,"* Dad says from across the breakfast table. He's wearing his fuzzy purple bathrobe, sipping from a chipped coffee mug.

"What?" I say.

"You're not chewing enough. Twenty chews per bite ensures maximum nutrient absorption. You need all your strength today."

"Is that supposed to be a pep talk?"

"I'm just saying."

I chew the banana until I've made a smoothie in my mouth, then swallow.

"So," I say. "You guys comin'?"

Despite all the grief my family causes me, I think deep down I really *do* want them to come. I know because when I fantasize about winning, they're always there, celebrating with me, game-show style.

"I mean, it doesn't matter," I add quickly. "It's up to you."

I feel like a conversation is an invisible tightrope sometimes. Two people have to wobble across it at the same time.

"*Of course* we want to be there," Dad says. "It's just . . . your mother and I were talking. We feel like . . . I don't know. We feel like sometimes we kind of . . . make you worse? So if you don't want us to come, we won't be offended."

"No," I say. "It's fine. You guys can come."

"*Great!*" He's so excited he almost chokes on his coffee. "I mean, uh, yeah, sounds good. You riding your bike over?"

"Yeah."

"Okay. We'll meet you over there."

"And *Franny*?" I say, peeling a second banana.

"What about him?"

"Can you make sure he doesn't . . . do anything Franny-like?"

My brother is a human tornado that wrecks things just to film himself doing it. I'm tempted to tie him up so he can't come anywhere near this race. It's too important.

Dad sighs. "Look. Your brother's worked very hard on

his YouTube channel. You know that. If he wants to film at the race, I don't think it'd be fair to—"

"Forget it," I say, peeling the rest of my banana, raising it toward my mouth.

"Your brother's his own person, son. We can't legislate his behavior."

"But you *can*. That's what parenting *is*."

"Not to us. You know that." To Dave and Diane Falloon, parenting isn't about *rules*. It's about Creating a Worldview That Will Allow Us to Decide Right from Wrong for Ourselves.

I toss my banana peel in the trash . . . and chew the final bite twenty times before racing out the back door.

REGIONAL QUALIFIER

Excerpted from ESPN's 30 for 30 documentary, "Crossing the Line: The Incredible True Story of the Million Dollar Race."

Grant Falloon, Track Star

The registration tent—man, it was crazy. There must've been like five hundred kids there. I guess you dangle a million bucks on your hook, you get a lotta fish.

Jay Fa'atasi, Track Star/Best Friend

It felt like the tryouts for *American Idol* or something. You know how you have the Actual Talented People? The ones with a real chance of winning? But then also the Delusional Ones who *think* they have talent but really don't? And then, of course, the Clowns, just there to make a mockery of everything and post it on their social media?

Grant Falloon, Track Star
We waited in line to register. I made fun of Jay because he'd brought all these extra documents—he practically had his second-grade spelling tests. We only needed the permission form at that stage.

Jay Fa'atasi, Track Star/Best Friend
Better safe than sorry, bro.

Grant Falloon, Track Star
At eleven fifteen a flex of dudes in EVENT STAFF T-shirts—

Jay Fa'atasi, Track Star/Best Friend
A *flex*?

Grant Falloon, Track Star
You know how a group of bats is a cauldron? And a group of crows is a murder?

Jay Fa'atasi, Track Star/Best Friend
Yeah.

Grant Falloon, Track Star
A group of security guards is a flex.

Jay Fa'atasi, Track Star/Best Friend
[Laughs.] I like that.

Grant Falloon, Track Star
So anyway, the guards wheeled out this
giant projector screen. By the time they
got the livestream working, the old lady
sponsoring the race, Ms. Babblemoney, was
already mid-sentence on the screen.

Jay Fa'atasi, Track Star/Best Friend
Babblemoney's one of those super-rich
people who wear the exact same thing
every day.

Grant Falloon, Track Star
Red tracksuit and pearls.

Jay Fa'atasi, Track Star/Best Friend
She looks like a sporty version of the queen
of England. [Laughs.]

Grant Falloon, Track Star

I was thinking about what she'd said in the announcement . . . about how champions don't let anything or anyone stand in their way.

Esther Babblemoney, Billionaire CEO

[On projector screen]
[Seated in what appears to be some kind of private library]
. . . always dreamed of something like this. . . . When I was your age, our parents shoved us out the door first thing in the morning. There was nothing else to do, so we all lined up to see who could run to the tree the fastest, who could throw this rock the furthest, who could jump over the creek . . .

Jay Fa'atasi, Track Star/Best Friend

She went on for like ten minutes, telling us about her whole childhood, blah blah. Finally the livestream cut out, and a track official in a red Babblemoney hat explained the rules. There would be a series of preliminary heats to weed out the riffraff. Then the top eight finishers would compete in a winner-take-all final.

Grant Falloon, Track Star

I was in the first heat.

Jay Fa'atasi, Track Star/Best Friend

Grant has always taken racing seriously. Like, maybe a little *too* seriously. That day he was *extra* focused.

Grant Falloon, Track Star

Yeah. When I get in that kind of zone, my vision shrinks to exactly forty-two inches— the width of my lane.

Jay Fa'atasi, Track Star/Best Friend

It's like he has lane vision instead of tunnel vision.

Grant Falloon, Track Star

It wasn't until just before the start that, out of the corner of my eye, I saw—

Jay Fa'atasi, Track Star/Best Friend

A turtle!

Grant Falloon, Track Star

[Shakes head.] The kid next to me was wearing a full-body turtle costume, the kind with the giant shell and everything. The kid's friends were all lined up along the fence outside the track, filming with their phones, laughing.

Diane Falloon, Mom
Grant didn't get off to the best start. It was like his Wi-Fi dropped out for a split second. Then he realized, *Oh, it started!*

Grant Falloon, Track Star
One of the worst starts of my *life*.

Jay Fa'atasi, Track Star/Best Friend
Even with the bad start, he still won his heat easily. It was like an NBA player playing in a high school game or something. He was just on a different level.

Diane Falloon, Mom
Grant had the best overall time for a while. . . .

Dave Falloon, Dad
Until Jay's heat.

Grant Falloon, Track Star
I watched him from way up high in the bleachers. I don't usually get that view. He

was *flying* down the track. I'd never realized how easy he makes it look. He had the best time so far. Easily.

Jay Fa'atasi, Track Star/Best Friend
There were eight of us in the final . . . but the other six lanes might as well have been empty. It was coming down to me and Grant. We knew it. Everyone knew it.

Grant Falloon, Track Star
Just before the race, when we were pacing around, shaking out our legs, I had this crazy idea. I was like, "Yo, we should tie."

Jay Fa'atasi, Track Star/Best Friend
I was like, "Wait. What? For real?"

Grant Falloon, Track Star
I was thinking about how we'd tied for last at the Penn Relays. What if we did the same thing, but tied for first. Would we *both* advance to nationals?

Jay Fa'atasi, Track Star/Best Friend
It was tempting, for sure. But I was like, "Bro, they'll just make us race again."

Grant Falloon, Track Star
He was right. Plus, even if we tried, it'd
be almost impossible. One of us would
accidentally cross first.

Jay Fa'atasi, Track Star/Best Friend
By the end of the race you're like a wave
washing up on the shore. It'd take a
superhuman effort to stop yourself.

Grant Falloon, Track Star
We both knelt in the blocks.
I closed my eyes.
Runners on your marks . . .
Set . . .

Jay Fa'atasi, Track Star/Best Friend
But the race didn't start. Something was
happening.

Grant Falloon, Track Star
It was hard to see what was going on.

Jay Fa'atasi, Track Star/Best Friend
Security guards came running onto the
track. I looked over at Grant. He was

shaking his head like *I can't believe this.*
Then I looked closer.

Grant Falloon, Track Star
My brother was lying across the finish
line with his ankle chained to a cinder
block. He was yelling through a bullhorn:
"Babblemoney owns your dreams!"

Diane Falloon, Mom
I knew what Franny was saying. How these
giant corporations, they create this vision
of what you're supposed to be . . . and then
cash in on it. Because to be that version of
yourself . . . you have to buy their product.

Dave Falloon, Dad
We've always taught the boys to stand up
and fight for what they believe.

Diane Falloon, Mom
But—I think we can agree—this was *not* the
appropriate forum.

Jay Fa'atasi, Track Star/Best Friend
Dude. The crowd was booing Franny so hard.

Grant Falloon, Track Star

Franny was loving it. The more they
booed—the more of a spectacle it became—
the better.

Jay Fa'atasi, Track Star/Best Friend

He was filming himself, of course. I was like,
"Bro, your brother's a genius. He's gonna get
so many views from that."

Grant Falloon, Track Star

They finally dragged Franny off the track.
I was stunned. I felt like I was watching
my life in the third person. And now I was
supposed to *race*?

Jay Fa'atasi, Track Star/Best Friend

I felt bad for Grant . . . but this wasn't the time
for a pity party.

Grant Falloon, Track Star

But then something really cool happened.
It was like things had become so ridiculous
that nothing mattered anymore. The tension
left my body. I felt great. I exploded out of
the blocks, arms firing like pistons. I felt my

spikes biting into the track, spitting it out. It was the best start of my life. *But still...*

Jay Fa'atasi, Track Star/Best Friend
I was right with you. [Smirks.]

Diane Falloon, Mom
I couldn't believe how fast they were moving. Both of them.

Dave Falloon, Dad
I was holding my breath the whole time.

Grant Falloon, Track Star
Our strides were perfectly in sync: left foot, right foot, left foot...

Jay Fa'atasi, Track Star/Best Friend
Mirror images.

Dave Falloon, Dad
I swear they crossed the line at the *exact* same time.

Diane Falloon, Mom
It really was that close.

Grant Falloon, Track Star
Afterward we paced on the track, hands atop our heads. We hugged. I said something like "Good race, bro. Good race." We still didn't know who'd won.

Jay Fa'atasi, Track Star/Best Friend
The judges were crowded around a little TV monitor.

Grant Falloon, Track Star
The judges all nodded, agreeing on something. One of them leaned over and said something to the PA announcer.

Kevin Casey, Public Address Announcer
Ladies and gentlemen (gentlemen) . . . today's winner (winner) . . . advancing to the national qualifier (qualifier) . . . is (is) . . .

Grant Falloon, Track Star
I stared down at my feet. I already knew. *This* was my destiny. To get inches from my dream. Only to—

Kevin Casey, Public Address Announcer
GRANT FALLOON.

Grant Falloon, Track Star

I couldn't believe it. I'd won. Jay came over and hugged me. We pressed our foreheads together. I don't think we even said anything.

Jay Fa'atasi, Track Star/Best Friend

I *had* to see the video, though. I went over to check the monitor.

Grant Falloon, Track Star

It's funny—as a sprinter, you're taught not to lean. Leaning causes deceleration. We all know that. But there I was in the freeze-frame, leaning over the line like a lowercase *r* . . .

Jay Fa'atasi, Track Star/Best Friend

It's crazy. All those years staring down, hunched over, embarrassed by your family. It won you the race!

Grant Falloon, Track Star

Leaving the track, I looked back over my shoulder. Jay was still there, crying onto his mom's shoulder. Seeing that . . . I don't know. Something, like, loosened in my

chest. My best friend—my *brother*—he was
hurting. I wanted to run back. I even started
to. But I couldn't. Going back would've
made it worse somehow, like I was gloating
or pitying him. I didn't even want him to
know that I'd seen.
So I just left.

10

Jay's basement. Sometime last summer. We're both in sleeping bags on the carpet. We like to sleep down here because we can stay up later. His mom made us turn off the TV, but it's still kind of glowing darkly, if that makes sense.

He says, "You awake, bro?"

"Nah," I say.

We both laugh.

"What's up?" I say.

"You ever get a song stuck in your head? I mean like really bad?"

"Dude. One time I had 'Baby Shark' in there for like a month. I thought I was gonna have to get my head amputated."

I sense his smile in the dark.

"That ever happen with anything else?" he asks. And now I know it wasn't a real question. It was just a question to get to the question.

He rolls toward me.

I roll toward him.

"How 'bout a dream?" he says. "You ever have a dream get stuck in your head? I have the same one every night."

"Really?"

"Yeah. It's . . . my brother."

"For real?"

"Yeah. He's on this mission in the desert . . . and he's hurt. He's reaching for me saying, 'Help. Please.' But I don't. I just stand there and watch."

"Did you tell your mom?" I ask.

"Come on, bro."

"What?"

"You think I need her worrying about me, too?"

I roll away so I'm flat on my back. I can't tell if I'm seeing the outline of the ceiling panels or projecting them from memory. I feel dumb. By comparison, all my family drama seems so small. "It's just a dream," I say. "He'll be fine."

"Yeah. I know. . . ."

A few minutes pass. We're both staring up at the ceiling. Finally he rolls toward me and whispers, "Baby Shark doot-doot, doot-doot-doot-doot, Baby Shark, doot-doot, doot-doot-doot-doot . . ."

I shove him. "Noooooooooo!"

We laugh so loud that his mom stomps on her bedroom floor, two levels up. Her don't-make-me-come-down-there warning stomps.

We cover our mouths and laugh quietly.

My family has this annoying tradition where, right before we eat, we go around and say a word that sums up our day. A single word. I've just won the regional championship, so for once I'm looking forward to the words they'll choose.

"*Proud,*" Mom says, steam rising from her plate.

"*Thrilled,*" Dad says, beaming.

"*Skeptical,*" Franny says—meaning about the Million Dollar Race in general, and we all frown, but he doesn't back down.

And now it's my turn.

I try on a few words in my mind, seeing how they feel. *Excited?* Definitely. But that doesn't quite capture it. *Invincible?* Nah, because I know how close I was to losing. If any one of a hundred tiny things had gone differently, I'd be choosing from a much darker collection of words. This is why my parents do this. It forces you to reflect.

"Relieved," I finally say.

Mom's smile flickers. "Relieved" means I *expected* myself to win, and anything less would've been a crushing disappointment. She's always saying how running should just be fun, the way it started. I blink, and she's smiling brightly again.

"Well cheers to our champion," she says, raising her bubbling seltzer.

After dinner I'm up in my room, reading about all the other regional winners on my phone. I peek up for a second, and Franny's in the doorway. He's leaning against the frame, holding his open laptop in his palm, long hair in a ponytail.

Aside from passing insults, we hardly ever talk anymore. In another lifetime, believe it or not, we were best friends.

"Hey," he says. "I just wanted to say . . . congrats. I think it's awesome that you won."

"Thanks," I mutter.

And that could be it.

It could be over.

But then I say, "But who really cares, right? You got your footage. That's all that really matters, right?"

To my own surprise, I *want* him to say something back. I want things to escalate until we scream at each other. I want fireworks, an explosion. Maybe if we burn it all down, something new could rise from the ashes.

Instead he opens his mouth like he's going to respond—then leaves.

11

Next morning, I'm on the fenced-in walking bridge over the highway. It's the midway point between my house and Jay's house. We meet here every morning, then jog over to the middle school track to train.

Except today . . . he's not here.

I check my phone.

No texts.

I start to write Yo bro, where u—

But I delete it.

What if he's not coming . . . on purpose?

What if, no matter how much we say "no hard feelings," it's impossible to be both rivals *and* best friends? I take a deep breath and grip the metal fence. The rust crumbles beneath my fingertips.

Below, the cars inch along in their dotted lanes. It's the most normal thing in the world. Morning traffic. And yet, if you tilt your head just slightly, it all seems *insane*.

Normal (n): You wake up every morning, pee, brush your teeth, shower, get dressed, and then go to some cramped, over-bright office, where you stay for the next eight hours, making someone else a lot of money.

Gripping the fence, I promise myself that I won't ever be like that—inching toward some finish line that I hate. No. I'll be a star. When I need to get somewhere, I'll have a private helicopter. Or better yet, the world will come to *me*.

I turn, and Jay's jogging toward me.

"My bad," he says, wearing all-white running gear with neon-yellow sneakers. "Couldn't sleep, then I overslept. Kinda funny when you say it out loud." He shrugs. "You know what I mean."

"It's all good," I say.

We fist-bump.

Jogging toward the track, we spot my brother outside the Town Watch building. We stop and observe him from a distance like he's an exhibit at the zoo. He's holding his phone up, saying something we can't hear.

Jay says, "You know how they say if you make a funny face for too long your face will get stuck like that?"

"Yeah?"

"I think his *arm* is gonna get stuck like that, in selfie-taking position."

I laugh. "It really is amazing. His whole life is just . . . content."

Jay smirks. "Yo, remember those lame movies you guys used to make?"

It's true. When we were kids, me and Franny had our own company: G&F Productions. We were a perfect creative duo because our personalities suited us to different roles. I was always the writer. I'd sit at Dad's typewriter and think up the weirdest, wildest plots. I loved the way the words would pour out of my fingertips and appear on the page with that awesomely loud *clack!*

Franny was the talent. He'd lounge beside the inflatable pool, in Mom's sunglasses, sipping lemonade, while I labored over the script. I'd rush out the back door, holding the new pages excitedly over my head, and he'd say, drowsily, "I hope this is better than your last effort."

My favorite movie was about a swashbuckling cowboy named Small Bladder Bill. He was always late to his gunfights because he had to stop to pee so many times on the way. We had to reshoot it like ten times because we were both laughing so hard. Something about being on camera made us so giggly.

It was still a novelty back then, I guess.

Watching Franny now, with the low drone of the highway behind us, I say to Jay, "Imagine if a young Einstein had been obsessed with getting views and likes instead of gazing up at the stars, wondering how it all works."

Jay frowns. "Bro, if there'd been social media back then, Einstein's ideas would've spread way faster and wider. It would've been awesome." He rubs his chin. He claims he's growing a goatee, but there's nothing there. "You really think Franny's *that* smart? Like, Einstein level?"

I don't know about *that*. But Franny's the smartest kid I know. He's probably smarter than all the rest of our family combined. (I would never admit this, of course.)

No, his intelligence has never been the question.

The question is if he'll use his powers for good or evil.

12

A week later it's Jay's mom's fortieth birthday party. Originally they were going to have it at their house, but then so many aunts and uncles and cousins RSVP'd that they had to rent the local church hall. It's a Samoan tradition that each branch of the family tree has to be represented for major celebrations.

I know it's silly, but I get nervous when our families are in the same place. I mean, it's fine. Mom and Dad love Mrs. Fa'atasi; she loves them. They always say, "We need to all get together more often!" But then they don't, and I'm glad. I guess I like to keep my two worlds separate—or rather, I've made a new world for myself, and I don't want my parents polluting it with their toxic weirdness.

I'm riding over early with the Fa'atasis to help them set up. With me and Jay in the back seat of his mom's Camry, it feels like she's our personal Uber driver. Which is kind of what a parent is, if you think about it.

(Minus the rating system.)

(That would be awesome.)

I'm staring out the window, daydreaming that I'm being interviewed on *ESPN*.

> **Interviewer:** Grant, thanks for making time to talk to us. We know you're super busy with all your endorsements and your charity work and your training.
>
> **Grant:** [Neck weighed down by gold medals] My pleasure.
>
> **Interviewer:** We have a lot of young viewers out there who tell us you're their hero, they want to be just like you. Can tell us what makes you so great?
>
> **Grant:** Well, *ESPN*, I have to tell you, there's no shortcut, no magic phone call that will make all your dreams come true. It's really all about hard work. Everyone says "follow your dreams". . . but to me, that's not good enough. I want to become so fast that my dreams have to struggle to keep up with me.

Interviewer: So, instead of following your dreams, you want your dreams to . . . follow you?

Grant: [Flashes million-dollar smile.] Exactly.

Fiddling with his seat belt, Jay says, "So I started doing some scouting. There's a kid from California who ran a 10.79. He's fast. But if you do your thing, you should dust him, no problem."

I ran a 10.76 at regionals, just shy of the record for our age group.

Jay ran a 10.77.

It's crazy how, in our world, a hundredth of a second can matter so much. It can change your future in major ways.

At a red light, Mrs. Fa'atasi eyes us in the rearview mirror. "What you clowns whispering about?"

"Just plotting our world takeover," Jay says.

She swats back playfully, then turns up her audiobook again. The light turns green.

"Been meaning to ask you," Jay says. "You thought about what you're gonna wear at nationals?"

I have to laugh. It's such a *Jay* question. First time I ever saw him, winter of fourth grade, just after he'd moved from Hawaii, he was running laps around our neighborhood in a designer coat. The faux-fur hood kept falling over his eyes.

I remember standing there by the window. A single snowflake had frozen to the upper corner of the glass. I remember watching this new kid go by again and again, never seeming to slow down, and I thought, *Who is this dude? Where'd he come from?*

"You should run track," I said the next day at school. I was thinking he'd be a great first leg for our 4x100 relay. "You're fast."

"I am?" he said, wide-eyed. "You really think?"

"Yeah, I—"

"I'm joking, bro. I know I'm fast. Are *you*?"

We both smirked.

It was only later that he told me *why* he'd been running all those laps. "Bro," he said. "I had to keep running, or I felt like I was gonna *die*."

Coming here from Hawaii (his mom had taken a job as the manager of a local warehouse), he'd never experienced winter before.

He'd only seen it on TV.

My favorite part of Samoan parties is the food. Everything's cooked in this underground oven called an *umu*. When the food comes out, all the juices have been swapping around, and it tastes (to quote Jay himself) "amazeballs." *Pisupo* (corned beef). *Palusami* (coconut shreds/milk/onions/fish). And so much more.

The church hall is decorated with traditional Samoan fine mats and strings of colored lights. I've already hit the buffet three times. I can't help noticing the tofu shrimp Mom brought hasn't been touched. She, Dad, and Franny are all on the dance floor, gyrating awkwardly to a Black Eyed Peas song.

"Dude," Jay says, heaping more pork onto his plate. "Your parents have some serious dance moves."

"Yeah," I say, face reddening.

"I mean, I've seen the robot before. But *tandem robot*? That's next level."

Mom is pretending to apply oil to Dad's creaky joints. Franny is their robot child—filming them.

"Something's up," Jay says, walking back to our table with his food.

"Huh?"

"I mean, with this party. My mom's acting weird, don't you think?"

"Seems pretty normal to me."

"I think she's got something up her sleeve."

"For her own party?"

Last year Mrs. Fa'atasi hired a full mariachi band to play "Happy Birthday" to Jay at his birthday dinner. She loves big, over-the-top gestures. It must be where Jay gets his love of the spotlight.

"Something's definitely up," he says.

A few minutes later the DJ plays "Lavalava Samoa" by the Five Stars. Jay rolls his eyes. "Bro, if I hear this song one more time . . ." But everyone flocks to the dance floor, and we follow. A circle forms, and Jay gets pushed into the center. He busts a few moves, and then one of his cousins jumps into the circle with him.

Except . . . it's not a cousin.

It's his older brother, Tua.

The Marine who's supposed to be in Afghanistan.

For what feels like an infinitely long second, Jay's shell-shocked. He stands in the center of the circle, arms at his sides, eyes welling with tears. Then he springs forward and hugs his brother super tight.

Everyone cheers.

"You're home!" Jay keeps saying, face pressed hard into Tua's chest. "You're home. You're *home*."

Mrs. Fa'atasi's sobbing, fanning herself with both hands, her boys reunited.

"A picture!" she says. "We need a picture!"

The Fa'atasis all drape their arms around one another, cheesing super bright. "Come on!" Mrs. Fa'atasi says, waving to me. "Come on! Get in the picture, Grant!"

"Me?" I say. "No. I'm fine. I'm—"

But she insists.

They all insist.

Probably no one else can tell, but I can—*it's my fake smile*. Like all my school portraits. I'm not doing it on purpose. I really am happy. Tua's home. He's safe. This is awesome. It's amazing. I guess I just feel awkward because I'm not *really* a member of their family, you know? I just like to pretend that I am.

We all dance for a while longer, and then it's time for

the best part—dessert. Tua eats a slice of cake with one arm draped around Jay's shoulder. You could see the affection between them from the moon.

"So," Tua says. "We gonna finish that game of Monopoly or what?"

"I kept it just the way we left it," Jay says. "I swear. I didn't touch it."

They do a secret brother handshake with slaps and snaps.

I have no idea what they're talking about.

My face must show it.

"The night before he left," Jay explains, "we were playing this epic game of Monopoly, but it wouldn't end. So we counted the money. I put the board under my bed so we could pick it up when he got back."

"That's awesome," I say, though suddenly I'm fidgeting, desperate to get out of here.

"You wanna sleep over?" Jay asks. "You can jump in the game. I'll give you half my money."

"That'd be awesome," I say. "But I, uh, I told my dad I'd help him with this project when we get home."

Jay tilts his head at the obvious lie.

"Your dad still make those dolls?" Tua says. It's the first thing he's said directly to me all night. "What were they? Dracula?"

I can't believe he remembers. I wasn't even sure he knew my *name*. His gold chain is hanging outside his plaid button-down shirt. It's like a god has come down from the heavens and is sitting here with us.

"Yeah," I say. "This is his busy season."

"That's cool," Tua says. "That's awesome. You guys are awesome."

"Grant's family is *very* creative," Mrs. Fa'atasi says, and I can tell she means it as a genuine compliment, but I still cringe inside.

The party ends, and the adults all hug goodbye. Mrs. Fa'atasi says, "Ah! So good to see you guys! Let's do it again soon!"

"We always say that!" Mom says. "But for real this time!"

"Yes! For real!"

I said before I have two different worlds—one at the Fa'atasis', one at home—but sometimes it feels like I have *none*. Nowhere I truly belong.

On the ride back I daydream about having my own private island again—my own sovereign country where I'm king. But until I win that million bucks, it can only exist in my mind.

"What are you smiling about?" Franny asks as we turn into our driveway.

"Nothing."

W hat do you see when you look at that?

    If you're like me, *not much*. It sort of looks like a piece of a beehive? Or a soccer ball? But to my parents, it's much more. They both have it tattooed on their inner wrists. They scribble it on the love notes they hide around the house for each other.

    They claim it's the exact chemical structure of their love.

    They met in ninth grade. Organic chemistry. That was the formula written on the board the first day.

    Their first "date" was in the school lunchroom (open-faced turkey, mashed potatoes, dirt-brown gravy). The conversation was so awkward, Mom says, that she opened her notebook, offered him a mechanical pencil from her twelve-pack, and said, "Let's both start drawing at the same time and see what we make."

(What they made has been lost to history.)

They dated all through high school. After graduation they drove cross-country in a beat-up minivan that looked like a spaceship. (This was before they swore off fossil fuels.) They moved to one of those "off-the-grid" hippie communes in northern California. Everyone was equal there. A pure democracy. It's the basis for our Family Council.

"We wanted to live outside the lines" is how Mom describes it. "We didn't see why our lives had to follow the same boring map as everyone else's, you know? That same dotted line—high school, college, work—leading to the big fat X at the end. So"—she reaches out and squeezes Dad's hand—"we made our own map."

"We both came from such small families," Dad says. "Driving out west to the commune, we had this crazy idea that could change the whole definition of a family. Make it bigger, more inclusive—why not, you know? That was our dream. Why does a family have to be just people you're related to by blood? Why do we have to do things the way everyone else does?"

I was born on September 14, 2008, in an old yellow school bus with all the seats ripped out. Mom was in labor for twenty-six hours, apparently.

"Only day in your life you weren't in a rush," Mom jokes.

I have this mental image of her—exhausted, sweaty—though obviously it can't be my own memory; I must've borrowed an image from a movie and swapped in her face.

I wonder how often we do that.

How much of our personal history is *pirated*.

The three of us lived on the commune until Mom got pregnant again.

"We loved it there," Dad says with a touch of sadness in his voice. "It really did feel like a big family. But we realized it wasn't the place we wanted to raise you guys. We didn't feel it was fair to force such a big choice onto you. So we took some of the big ideas and brought them home with us, the best of both worlds."

Which Mom translates as "We got tired of pooping in the woods."

Dad uses our garage as his Dracula production studio. It's always super dark, lit only by electric jack-o'-lanterns and occasional bolts of fake lightning. The creepy atmosphere (fake cobwebs, fog machine, high-pitched evil laughter) gets him in the zone, he says, which as an athlete I can respect. He's the number four producer of custom Halloween tchotchkes on the East Coast.

I flick on the lights. Now it just looks like a cluttered garage. The boxes he ships the dolls in—custom-designed like little coffins—are stacked up on the far wall.

He's not in here.

Back inside, Mom's in her office, surrounded by law books, reading glasses on the tip of her nose.

"I need your help with this registration stuff," I say. "The national qualifier has more paperwork."

"Oh, your father's really the one for that."

I have trouble believing he's the one for anything.

You know, except *her*.

I finally find him down by the gas station on Ridge Avenue. He's doing one of his weird community-art projects. When he's not making Halloween stuff, his "day job," he designs "interactive experiences."

For example:

Today he's taped the front page of the newspaper to a bus shelter. A picture of the president touring some kind of natural disaster. Beneath it he's taped a blank sheet of paper labeled COMMENT SECTION with blank boxes for people to write their thoughts. A pen dangles from a string.

It's sneakers-melting-on-the-asphalt hot out here. Dad's already sweat through his white V-neck. Seeing me, he tips up his fedora and smiles. "What's this?" I say.

"I call it Real World Comment Section. What would happen, it asks, if we took the toxic, divisive, anonymous discourse we find online and made it public? What happens if, instead of hiding behind a screen, you have to declare what you think in front of your neighbor in a shared public space?"

"I need your help," I say.

"*Exactly*," he says. "That's just it. When forced to express yourself in a public space, it immediately makes you vulnerable. It says, implicitly, *I need your help.* You need *my* help. We're both in this—"

"No. Dad. *I* need *your* help. Like, right now."

"Oh. What's up?"

"I can't find my birth certificate."

"Birth certificate?"

"You know. The *cer-tif-i-cate?* That *certifies your birth?*" I let the words hang in the sticky-hot air. He's still standing next to the bus shelter, hands on hips.

"I need it to register at nationals," I say.

"Why?"

Ugh. His favorite question. With Mom and Dad there's always this built-in layer of skepticism. They've tried to pass it on to us, but it's not necessarily genetic. Sometimes I just want to take things at face value. It's exhausting to question *everything.*

Dad wears homemade deodorant ("You know what kind of chemicals they put in that stuff?"). It isn't working. He reeks like boiled onions. He blots his forehead with the sleeve of his T-shirt. "I have to tell ya, son. If I'm being honest, I do kind of resent the whole idea of"—he makes air quotes—*"birth certificates."*

Here we go.

"I mean, what does a silly piece of paper tell me that my

eyes can't? You *exist*. There you are. A miraculous, living, breathing feat of nature who presumably didn't appear out of thin—"

"Dad."

He runs his hand through his greasy hair and puffs out his cheeks. "I think it's in the attic. Come on. I'll help you look."

15

Attics are funny, if you think about it. It's like every family builds a time capsule and buries it in the lowest part of the sky.

Dad reaches up and pulls the knotted string hanging from the ceiling. The hatch unfolds into a wooden ladder. "After you," he says.

This time of year—last week of July—it's like a sauna up here. Dust motes are swimming by the lone circular window. First thing I see (it really draws the eye) is a massive plaster sculpture of my parents when they were teenagers.

Dad's standing behind Mom, prom-pose style. They've both got talons and wings like they're fearsome mythical creatures. I recognize it as an amazing work of art . . . but that doesn't mean I wanna *look at it*.

I mean, they're *nude*.

What kid wants to look at his parents naked? What's the point of winning the trust fund if I have to blow the whole thing on therapy?

Dad—still in his sweat-drenched T-shirt—crouches beneath the sloped ceiling. He opens a cardboard box labeled KIDS' ART. He digs for a minute and unearths a family portrait I must've made when I was five. We're all stick figures. Mom. Dad. Grant. Franny. The lines of our arms are connected, signaling that we're holding hands. We're all smiling. The paper crinkles like a dead leaf.

"It might be in that one," he says, nodding to a box behind me.

I tug open the cardboard flaps and look inside.

I'm six years old. Still gangly and freckle-faced, but not so hunched over yet. Alone in our kitchen, I reach up and pin a piece of loose-leaf paper on the fridge—two magnets just to be safe. I smile at my work. Front teeth missing.

TOP 5 THINGS GRANT WANTS FOR HIS BIRTHDAY
1. Captain America action figure (New)
2. Captain America action figure (New)
3. Captain America action figure (New)

4. Captain America action figure (New)

5. Captain America action figure (Fine, I'll take a used one)

The Avengers are super popular right now. Even our teacher, Mr. Mack, has an Iron Man key chain. It's like a CGI religion.

When the big day finally arrives, I race home from school, book bag bouncing on my shoulders. We have pizza from Frank's (mmmm) and homemade vegan angel food cake for dessert (can't win 'em all). Mom, Dad, and Franny sing an out-of-tune "Happy Birthday" and then . . . nothing. No gift. I shouldn't be surprised. They're always going on about the Toy-Industrial Complex. . . .

But still . . .

I thought maybe . . .

"I'm tired," I say, softly pushing in my chair. "I'm going up to bed."

I mope up to my room . . . and that's when I see it. This action-figure-shaped box at the foot of my bed. Wrapped in butcher paper and yarn.

I can't believe it!

My heart is pounding. Yes! Yes yes yes! I race over and rip it open. Mom and Dad—who, I have to say, have set this up perfectly—are behind me, leaning in the doorway, smiling. And then . . .

"What's this?" I say, shedding the paper.

"A new action figure!" Dad says. "Just like you wanted!"

Um, did they not see the list? The very specific list? This is a doll. A homemade doll. Glued-on buttons for eyes. Real human hair.

"What's 'NVM'?" I say, frowning at the nail-polish lettering on the chest.

"It's NON-VIOLENT MAN!" Dad says. "Pull the string in the back!"

"Pull it!" Mom says giddily.

It's a wonky recording of Dad's voice, rasped real low like Batman. It says, "Let's make a better world . . . through kindness."

"And look!" Mom says. "When you pull the lever, he gives hugs!"

"Awwwwwwwwesome!" Franny says, crashing into the room. He rips the doll out of my hands. "This is so—"

Lame, I think, burying Non-Violent Man deep in the cardboard box. This is why I never come up here. This stuff is like emotional quicksand.

"Dad," I say. "Can we *please* find this stupid birth certificate?"

He's smelling an old crayon drawing of our house. "Yeah," he says. "Sorry. I just love all this stuff. You guys are so talented."

Of course it's in the very last box, way in the corner. An eight-by-eleven manila envelope labeled BIRTH CERTIFICATE/GRANT.

"You'd better check," I say.

"Huh?"

"To be sure there's actually something *in* there."

He peeks in.

"Yup," he says, flashing a thumbs-up, "all good."

And he reseals the envelope.

Because we don't have a car, we have to ride up to New York on this horrible bus called the Discount Rider. We make it just in time and have to sit in the very back, where it reeks like blue toilet water. The guy across the aisle is wearing a chicken costume for some reason, eating soup out of a ziplock bag.

"Would it have been *so* bad to rent a car?" I say.

"The electric ones were all sold out," Dad says. "Plus they're too expensive."

"The Wi-Fi isn't working," Franny says.

"This is dumb," I say. "Think how much carbon this bus is spewing out."

"Yeah," Mom says, "but this bus would be *running either*

way. If we rented a car, we'd be adding to what is already a very serious problem. Future generations will look back on us and say—"

"Yeah, yeah," I say.

"I'm *serious*," she says, turning to fully face me. "This is important. Sometimes you have to take a stand in life. Even if it's hard. Even if it makes your life a little less convenient. I hope when that day comes, you'll listen to your conscience instead of all the voices saying *gimme, gimme, gimme*."

Registration's in this old armory building in New York. I guess it used to be filled with tanks and bombs, but now it's a state-of-the-art athletic center.

The Babblemoney company logo, a golden *B* with a vertical line through it like a dollar sign, is everywhere. From the way I'm bouncing on my toes, you'd think I was nervous. But really I just want to get away from my parents.

"Oh hey," I say. "Looks like they have free coffee over there. . . ."

Mom takes the hint. "You have all your paperwork?" she asks.

"Yeah."

"Okay, text us if you need us."

She mouths *good luck* and drags Dad away.

Franny follows, arm up high like a submarine's periscope, filming the crowd.

I look around for a few seconds, taking it all in. It's pretty cool: Of the thousands of kids who competed at regionals, only the best of the best made it here to New York.

And I—Grant Falloon—am one of them.

Heading for the registration table, I spot a familiar face—*Jay!* He cuts diagonally across the crowd. We hug extra tight. "What are you doing here?" I say.

"Had my bro drive me up to surprise you!" he says. "You think I'd miss this?"

Tua's behind him. The sleeves of his T-shirt are rolled up on his tattooed arms. He gives me a fist bump and a smile. "Good luck, little bro! You got this!"

Hearing that—from *him*—gives me such a rush.

The three of us wait in the A–F registration line. Finally, I give the lady my PPF (parental participation form) and my birth certificate. She runs her finger down a list until she finds *FALLOON, GRANT*. I'm weirdly relieved. She makes a photocopy of the birth certificate and hands me back the original. "Just need your parents to sign this image release form and you're all set." She passes me the document. It says:

> I hereby give permission for images of my child, captured during the MILLION DOL-LAR RACE through video, photo, and digital

camera, to be used solely for the purposes of BABBLEMONEY COMPANY promotional material and publications, in perpetuity, and waive any rights of compensation or ownership thereto.

"What's 'in perpetuity' mean?" I ask.

"Forever," the woman says, smiling.

"So, like, you own my image forever?"

"As it relates to this event? Yes."

I look around. Everyone else's parents are signing the form. "I'll be right back," I say. "Just need to find my parents. Mind if I take this pen?"

"No problem! I'll be here!"

I take the form into a dark corner by some vending machines . . . and I forge Mom's signature.

Jay frowns. "What are you doing, bro?"

"They already said I could race. What's the big deal?"

"Isn't it a little weird that they want to own your image forever?"

"This is how it works in the big time," I say confidently, though of course I have no clue how it works in the big time.

I'd sign *anything* right now if it meant I could compete.

The Sneaker Queen's up on a platform in her famous red tracksuit and pearls.

"Boys and girls!" she says, wireless microphone shaking slightly in her bony hand. "Boys and girls! Welcome! Oh, what a dream come true! To see all your bright shining faces! The very best of the best! The cream of the crop!"

We dutifully applaud.

The harsh lighting in the athletic center is making Babblemoney look almost transparent, like a reflection on water. "As you may know," she says shakily, "I don't have any children or grandchildren. My whole life has been invested in this company. I've worked hard, yes, but I've also been fortunate. I feel it is my *duty* to give back. Just a few weeks from now, our very special winners—one boy and one girl—will receive a trust fund worth *one million dollars!*"

I turn to Jay, eyes wide.

Someone lets out a *whoop!*, and we all cheer wildly.

17

Nationals are just like regionals: a series of prelims, then the top eight compete in a winner-take-all final. The big difference, of course, is that it's indoor. In a way, actually, that could favor me. No wind to worry about, no rain, no distractions.

Well, I spoke too soon.

Up in the bleachers, Mom (who's painted a red G on her cheek) counts, "One, two, three!" She throws up her hands. Beside her, Franny throws up his hands. Then Jay, who's sitting with them. Then Tua. Then Dad, who, after completing their mini wave, cups his hands and yells, "Goooo, Grant! Yaaaaaaay sports!"

The kid next to me says, "Did that guy just yell . . . 'yay sports'?"

"I think he did," I say.

"You know him?"

"Nope."

I do my prerace stretches and am just heading to the track when, over the public address system, I hear two bone-chilling words: "GRAAAANT FAAAAALLOON."

I freeze. My whole body goes numb.

"GRAAAANT FAAAALLOON. PLEEEEASE REEEE-PORT TO THE REEEGISTRAAAATION AAAAREA IMMEEEEDIATELY."

Someone goes, "Oooooo," like I've just been summoned to the principal's office.

Everyone laughs. Everyone stares.

What the heck is happening?

A security guard leads me down a narrow hallway, into a room marked STAFF ONLY. It's some sort of conference room—a long rectangular table with chairs all around it. Blank gray walls. It smells like a Band-Aid.

A woman in a navy suit is waiting in a crisp white Babblemoney hat. *A lawyer.* She forces a pinched smile, hands folded on the table.

Mom and Dad and Franny rush into the room.

Jay and Tua close behind.

"What's going on?" Mom says, breathless.

"I'm afraid we have a problem," the lawyer says. She holds up the copy of my birth certificate. "I'm afraid this paperwork is . . . *insufficient*."

"What do you mean?" Mom says.

"I'm afraid"— the lawyer's tone softens when she peeks at me—"you won't be allowed to compete today."

You wouldn't think that a few sound waves passing through the air could make such an impact. But those words—"you won't be allowed to compete today"—they knock me back against the wall.

That's when the founder of the race, Esther Babblemoney, glides into the room on her electric scooter.

"What's the *meaning* of this?" she yells at the lawyer.

And already I feel better.

She's got my back.

She'll make this right.

The lawyer shuffles some papers. "Ms. Babblemoney. I was just, uh, saying. There's a problem with this young man's paperwork. We caught it just in time." The lawyer turns stiffly to Mom and Dad. "Mr. Falloon. Mrs. Falloon. When your son was born, did they give you this certificate at the hospital?"

"Our son wasn't born in a hospital," Dad says.

Please don't get defensive, Dad.

Just fix this.

"Right," the lawyer says. "So it was . . . a home birth?"

Dad explains about the commune in California.

The lawyer's glasses are hanging from a chain. She lifts them onto her nose. "It says here the witness was someone named . . . Karl?"

"Dr. William Karl?" Babblemoney says. "From Berkeley?"

"No," the lawyer says. "Just . . . Karl."

"Yeah," Dad says. "Sure. Yeah. Karl. He was there." He looks at Mom urgently. "Remember? He's the one who had the certificate made. Right?"

The lawyer frowns. "You can't just *make* your own birth certificate, Mr. Falloon. We need a legally certified document from the State of California."

"*Why?*"

"Because this is an international competition. There can only be one qualifier from each country, and each contestant must be the age they claim to be. This was all made very clear in the terms and conditions. Did you not read them?"

Dad throws his hands up and laughs defensively. "Oh *come on*! You want people to read that stuff you should have to provide microscopes!"

"As a matter of fact," the lawyer says, "I *do* expect people to 'read that stuff.' That's why I write it."

Mom—the lawyer—is staring down at the floor, shaking her head. Jay and Tua are pressing their backs against the wall, trying to make themselves invisible.

Franny's filming (of course).

I feel the moment slipping away. . . .

18

"Wait," I say, panic rising in my throat. "This is crazy. I've never even *seen* a birth certificate!"

And honestly—why would I? Has anyone my age? Our generation barely knows what a document *is*. Everything's online. I'd have to go to a museum or something. And now this stupid thing—a piece of paper—is going to decide my whole fate?

"I'm thirteen," I say, "I promise you. I'm American. I just don't have the paper. Can you *please* just make an exception? *Please?*"

I'm saying all this directly to Ms. Babblemoney, I realize, my hands clasped like I'm praying. Which I guess I sort of am.

Parked beside a fake fern on her electric scooter, Babblemoney's using all her strength to try to wrench open a sports drink bottle, blue veins pulsing in her neck. Feeling the weight of the room tipping toward her, she looks up. "What now?"

I repeat my heartfelt plea.

It seems to connect. Her red-rimmed eyes are watery. She folds her hands primly on her lap, lifts her chin, and says, very formally, "*No.*"

"Huh?" I say.

"I'm sorry," she says, brow raised. "But I'm afraid my stance on paperwork is *quite* firm."

Mom can't take it anymore. She goes full Lawyer Mode. "Listen," she says. "We don't want to fight you, lady. We're just saying . . . can't we use a little common sense here? You've got these kids' dreams in the palm of your hand. Maybe you don't take that seriously. But you should. My son hasn't done anything wrong. Don't penalize him for our mistake. He's a good kid. He worked hard to be here."

"I *don't* . . . *doubt* . . . *that*," Babblemoney says, trying again to open the sports drink bottle. Finally an assistant opens it for her. She takes a birdlike sip. "But think about it from *our* perspective. If we, the sponsoring organization, turn a blind eye to a matter like this . . . well *then* what? What happens next? I'll tell you. *Chaos.* It's like dominos. Tip one over, and it hits the next, and it hits the next . . ."

"But—"

"There must be *rules* in life," the old lady says, driving the scooter the long way around the conference table. It's the slowest scooter I've ever seen, like a toy car running out of batteries. "Hard lines that *cannot* be crossed. Maybe your little family here doesn't believe that. You color outside the lines. I see that. Okay. Fine. Good for you. "

She stops the scooter directly in front of Mom. "But guess what? Little news flash for you, missy. We're not living in your world. *You're living in mine.* So don't you come here, to *my* event, and presume to tell me right from wrong."

It's clear now that Babblemoney's got a sort of Dr. Jekyll and Ms. Hyde thing going on. *Except the opposite.* Under the bright camera lights, she's a sweet, harmless grandma. The rest of the time she's a monster, barely able to contain her rage.

To her credit, Mom keeps her composure.

What she does, in fact, is laugh.

Babblemoney doesn't like that. She glares at Mom, then turns to me and says, "Let this be a lesson to you, young man. If we don't have *rules*, we have *nothing.* My daddy taught me that a long time ago, and it's served me well. It's not too late for you to go on and make something of yourself."

"Easy for *you* to say," Dad scoffs. "You don't like a rule, you just pay a few million bucks to have it changed—then you act like it's been chiseled in stone since the beginning of time. You dangle a dollar on a hook, and all us suckers chase it around while you pick our pockets and call it 'fair.' Those are the 'rules.'"

Something about that amuses Babblemoney. She transforms back into the sweet grandma. She rubs the pearls hanging over her red tracksuit. "I just *hate* that you came all this way," she says, delivering each word with devastating politeness. "It's just *terrible*. But, as I said, rules are rules. I'm afraid I must get back to the competition now. This matter is closed. Your district will have no—

"*Waaaaait!*" I say.

I don't even know what I'm going to say until I say it.

"This is our alternate," I say, pointing to Jay. "Jay Fa'atasi. He finished second at regionals. He's here. He's ready. He'll take my spot."

"And *you* have the proper paperwork?" Babblemoney says to Jay.

Jay looks at me.

He mouths, *You sure, bro?*

I nod.

"Yeah," Jay says. "I think I actually still have all my stuff in the car from regionals."

"And the image release?" the lawyer says. "Signed by a parent or guardian?"

"I can . . ." He peeks at Tua, then at me. "I . . . can get that signed for you."

Against the wall, Tua crosses his arms.

But he doesn't say anything.

He lets Jay make his own choice.

I really don't think it's that big a deal—forging a release form.

Mrs. Fa'atasi would sign it if she were here, right?

"Very well," Babblemoney says, looking around, eyebrows raised, like she's done us all a great favor. "Then our little problem is solved."

19

It's an experience I've had so few times in my life—the feeling of falling behind, the pack leaving me in the dust.

And I hate it.

I hate it so much.

Hours later, I'm still here in the soulless conference room. I won't abandon Jay and leave the venue completely, but I can't show my face out there. I can't bear the stares. Every few minutes a cheer bleeds through the wall. I'm following online and know that the final race is about to start.

Mom, Dad, and Franny are on the other side of the long conference table, keeping their distance. Dad clears his throat. "Son, I just wanted to say . . . I think it needs to be said . . . that what you did earlier was . . . *honorable*."

"What?"

"Giving your spot to Jay like that."

"Great," I snap. "Well maybe I can compete for Honor-slovakia!"

Franny laughs—a little *too* hard. He pounds the table, cracking up.

I glare.

"What?" he says—still filming of course. "It was funny!"

I can't take it anymore. I leave the room and stomp back down the hall into the athletic center. Instead of everyone staring at me, like I expect, something even worse happens. *No one notices me at all.*

Jay's made it to the final. He's in lane five. I widen my eyes, trying to get his attention via Best Friend Telepathy. But it's too crowded in here. The signal is jammed. I'm as invisible to him as I am to everyone else.

As the race starts, the other seven kids have their Ugly Running Faces in full effect. Wide-eyed. Desperate. But the look on Jay's face is almost serene. I marvel at his long, effortless strides. He's doing it. He's pulling ahead.

Watching him cross the line, watching him leap joyously into Tua's arms, I feel bad that I almost kept him from having this moment.

It's a long bus ride home. Somewhere in New Jersey, I lock myself in the dark, smelly bathroom.

I've been having this problem for a while now that only seems to be getting worse as I get older. The problem is *I can no longer feel just one thing at a time.* The pure days of childhood, when I could experience a single emotion and not, like, see around the edges of what I'm feeling are gone.

All I want right now, hiding in this bathroom, is to be angry, to be livid, to be *freaking furious,* but I also feel bad, because I know my parents didn't mean for any of this to happen. They're devastated too.

All I want is to text my best friend, tell him, *You did it, bro. I knew you could. I'm proud of you!* But a part of me is resentful and bitter that he just won what should've been *mine.*

All these feelings, colliding at once. The net result is a hazy numbness that starts behind my eyes and spreads down through my whole body.

I don't remember when I started crying. But it's all pouring out now. Snot's bubbling out of my nose. My throat catches. It hurts so bad, but, in a weird way, I find myself balling up, *holding on to the pain.*

It's as close to a pure feeling as I can get.

"You okay?" Dad says when I sit down again.

I stare absently out the window. "I'm fine."

20

Next morning I'm sprawled on the picnic table outside Frank's Pizza, tossing a tennis ball up to myself. Above, through the wavy heat lines, the birds look like they've melted to the telephone wires. The plastic Coke sign has faded bubblegum pink.

"Not sure if you heard," the owner says, sticking his head out the side window, leaning on the ledge. "But this ain't a hotel."

I sit up slowly. "My bad."

"Where's your friend?"

Jay's brother took him to get celebratory pizza at Lorenzo's on South Street. I don't mention this to Frank. I don't want to make him jealous. I just shrug.

Frank dabs his pencil on his tongue and flips to a fresh page on his notepad. "What'll it be then? More grilled chicken?"

"I'm not really hungry," I say. "You mind if I just hang?"

"Sorry, kid. You know the rules. No loitering." He nods to a broom leaning against the wall. "But if you're *workin'*, that's different. . . ."

I push some stray pizza crusts around on the sidewalk for a while, thinking about Jay. About how our destinies were always joined. But now I'm stuck here, *disqualified*, and he's racing off to fame and glory without me.

Just when I feel like I've hit rock bottom, my brother comes oozing up the sidewalk. It's weird to see him without his phone in his hand, like an action figure without its weapon. "What are you doing?" he says.

"Oh hey," I say, pretending I just saw him. "Forgot to tell you. Kylie Jenner called last night. She wants her haircut back."

"Very funny."

"What do you want, Franny?"

"I've been looking for you."

"Well congrats. You cracked the case."

"We need to talk."

"Go ahead. It's a free country."

He looks both ways, like we're being watched, then says, "I think I found a way to fix this for you."

I set the broom against the brick wall, dust my hands. "Fix *what*?"

He leans away from the fly-swarmed trash bins and pinches his nose. "It's *nasty* out here. Meet me at my office in an hour."

I'd roll my eyes—

But it's too hot, and he's not worth the effort.

Franny's "office" is just a corner of his bedroom. On the walls he's taped up replicas of all the awards he plans to win someday—the Nobel Peace Prize is the centerpiece. His feet are up on his trash-picked IKEA desk, big toe sticking out of a hole in his sock.

"Listen," I say in the doorway. "I don't know what you're up to. I honestly don't care. But can you just . . . do it quickly?"

He opens his laptop and types his super-long password. The only folder on the desktop says *TOP SECRET*. Which, to me, seems like a dumb thing to label a top secret folder. Inside the folder are dozens of video files, documents, and spreadsheets.

He's been hard at work on *something*.

He says, "Did you ever go back and read those terms and conditions?"

"What terms and conditions?"

"On your sign-up sheet. For the race."

"Of course not. Why would I?"

He sighs. "This generation—*ugh*. Nobody *reads* anymore."

I grit my teeth to keep from smacking him.

He pedal-wheels his chair across the carpet—pausing briefly to untangle some dirty socks from the wheels—and closes the door. Like we're having some kind of secret meeting. Like *we*—me and him—are a team.

"Pop quiz," he says.

"Great. Just what I want in the summer."

"How many countries are there on earth right now?"

I'm just curious enough to play along. "Fifty?"

"Hundred and ninety-five."

"Wow. Really?"

He points to the world map on his wall. "And of those hundred and ninety-five, guess how many existed a *thousand* years ago, by today's standards?"

"Twelve?"

"Zero. They all vanished, or transformed into different versions of themselves."

"Great," I say. "Thanks for the history lesson."

"Now let me ask you this," he says, pacing with his hands behind his back like he's giving a TED Talk. "If the map looked completely different a thousand years ago, despite having the exact same landmasses . . . what do you think it'll look like *a thousand years from now?*"

"I have no idea."

"Exactly. None of us do. How could we? How could someone back in 1000 AD have predicted the United States? In Europe, they didn't even know North America *existed.* The map will completely transform again."

"What's your *point*?" I say.

"My point is . . . in the long view . . . the concept of a nation-state is actually pretty flimsy. You might even say it feels a little . . . made up."

It feels the opposite of that, I think. There are borders. Fences. Signs. Guards. The lines couldn't be more clear. They're right on the map.

"My *point*," he continues, raising his eyebrows dramatically, "is you have this once-in-a-lifetime opportunity here. All you have to do is reach out and grab it."

21

frown. "Some stupid online petition isn't going to change anything, Franny."

"I'm not *talking* about a petition," he says, voice charged with excitement that actually feels genuine. "We need to do something *bigger*. If you can't represent America . . . *why not just be your own country?*"

"Ha."

"I'm serious. Tell me why not?"

"Well, for starters—setting aside the fact that I don't own any *land*—which would make it hard to start a *country*—the competition is in—"

"Two weeks. Three hundred and thirty-four hours. That's plenty of time. All you need is to pick a name, make a flag, a few other small details. I mean, if your country can't produce some official letterhead in two weeks, we should just close up shop now. . . ."

"*We?*"

"Well naturally you'll need someone you trust to set up the IP address, since I assume this will be a digital territory."

"Digital?"

"Yup. We'll put your country online. It'll be everywhere and nowhere at the same time. All you need is Wi-Fi and you're there!"

I have to admit . . . for about a half second . . . I'm intrigued.

I mean, what even *is* a country?

A bunch of lines on a map? A group of humans who all happen to have been born in the same geographic area, with no say in the matter whatsoever?

Isn't that sort of random?

Why did I never question that before?

But then I crash back to reality.

"*No,*" I say, eyeing the dirty socks on his floor. "No way. Babblemoney will never go for it."

"But she will! She *will*! Trust me! All she cares about is—"

"Cut the crap, Franny. What's your angle here?"

"Angle?"

"Why do you want this so bad?"

He clutches his heart. Wounded. "But Grant. I'm your *brother. . . ."*

I laugh. "You think I'm gonna fall for that? Anything you've ever done has been to help *yourself.*"

He stares out the window, chewing the inside of his cheek. When he turns back, it's weird. It's like my little brother—the mop-haired boy I used to make silly movies with in the backyard, who used to bring bright pink poster boards to my track meets saying THAT'S MY BROTHER!!!— he's back.

"You know why you can trust me?" he says. "Because you're right. I *am* doing this for myself. All these years, while you're out there winning races, the golden boy . . . I've been in here *working*, making these stupid videos . . . knowing that one day I'd use this platform for an *actually* worthy cause. Well, up in New York I realized the answer was right there in front of me all along." He points. "It's *you.*"

"*Me?*"

"We can do this," he says, practically vibrating with excitement. "I'm telling you. Even if the idea is ridiculous— which it is, clearly—it's built on top of something real. We're all online these days . . . these digital versions of ourselves . . . kings and queens of our own domains. The physical place you were born—that's the old way of thinking!"

I tap my finger on my bottom lip, excited about this idea but also remembering our family motto. "Skepsis!" Question everything.

"How would it work?" I ask.

"Simple. We make a vlog about your quest to enter the competition. We tell your story—the scrappy underdog following his dream. We build subscribers . . . but instead of subscribers we call them your citizens. We use the existing infrastructure of social media . . . but transform it into something totally new!"

"I still don't see how this helps me get into the race," I say.

Franny closes his eyes and pinches the bridge of his nose. He gets frustrated when people can't see twelve moves ahead like he does. "Just trust me, okay? With my help, we'll grow your presence—your country—so big that Babblemoney will recognize the PR potential . . . and she'll let you in. This is all just one big commercial for her anyway."

"What do you mean?"

"Forget it. Just focus on what we can do *right now*."

I look over at his fake Nobel Prize on the wall. His falling-apart IKEA desk. I'm scared to trust him . . . but I find myself believing in what he's saying. What's really happening? Do I just want this so badly that I'm willing to grasp at any wisp of hope, even if it might vanish from my hands and make all this hurt even more? Or is he really onto something? I say, "You remember what Babblemoney said in New York?"

"Funny you should mention that."

He has the video queued up on his computer.

He plays it:

"But guess what? Little news flash for you, missy. We're not living in your world. *You're living in mine.* So don't you come here, to *my* event, and presume to tell me right from wrong."

"That was messed up," Franny says. "You don't talk to Mama Falloon like that."

"No," I say. "You don't."

We had a secret brother handshake once, I think. But I've long-forgotten it. The only history between us is ancient. If we're going to do this, we'll have to build atop the ruins. "I'm in," I say, extending my hand. "How do we start?"

22

At first we develop our plan in secret. We need to work out the bugs, or it could flop. But pretty soon we realize we're gonna need help. It's not like we—a thirteen- and a twelve-year-old—can just sneak out of the house and fly to California.

The first person I tell—no surprise—is Jay.

> G: hey bro
> G: so this is gonna sound weird . . .
> G: but franny had this idea 2 get me into the babblemoney race by starting our own country

J: uh
J: what

        G: he thinks it can work
        G: and i kinda do too

J: how can u just start a country
J: don't u need like . . . land

        G: we're gonna put it online

J: lol

        G: no im serious

J: bro that's genius!
J: i mean it's nuts
J: but who knows
J: if anyone could pull it off it's franny
J: wut ur parents say

        G: didn't tell 'em yet . . .

Next morning me and Franny call a Family Council.

"Mom, Dad," I say, standing in front of the fish tank in the living room. "Thank you for joining us today." I'm wearing mesh shorts, a T-shirt, slip-on sandals. Franny's wearing an oversize thrift store suit, blue with a red tie.

Mom's legs are bouncing with excitement. This is only the second time her boys have ever cosponsored something.

"We realize this is unusual," I say. "The two of us up here. *Together.*"

"For years we've backstabbed each other," Franny says. "Torn each other down at every opportunity. And what good has it ever done? Where has it ever gotten us?"

"Nowhere," I say.

"After what happened in New York," he says, "we realized it was time to set aside our differences—"

"Reach across the aisle—"

"Come together, work for the common good—"

"A house divided against itself cannot stand," I say.

Nailed it.

Mom applauds. *"See!"* she says, elbowing Dad. "I told you they'd work things out! Sometimes it just takes a little adversity to bring—"

"Now wait just a minute," Dad says.

Oh boy. Here we go.

"This is great, boys. Really. It's exciting. It's *beautiful.* But it all seems a bit . . . abrupt. Why do I get the sense that you two are up to something?"

"We are," Franny says, grinning. "We absolutely are."

He distributes the Information Packets.

"The way everything went down in New York,"

he explains, "it really bothered me. So I did a little research, wondering if maybe there might be a way to make things right. Turns out in the terms and conditions of the Million Dollar Race it states: 'There shall be one participant from each country.' What it doesn't specify—anywhere—is how many countries are *eligible* to enter or, more broadly, what even *defines* a country. We believe this leaves the matter open to interpretation."

I translate: "Yeah. So we're gonna start our own country. We're gonna crash the party, force them to let us in, and fly home with that million bucks."

"A digital country," Franny explains, "the very first of its kind. We're excited, but we need your help. Mom, we need your eyes on the legal stuff. Dad, we have lots to design. We wanna build this thing from the ground up!"

Mom and Dad are shoulder to shoulder on the lime-green couch. They look at each other. I can tell they love the idea, but they're fighting it. *Skeptical.*

"You know how you guys moved to the commune?" I say, trying a new tactic. "Because you wanted to expand the definition of family? This is like that. But even bigger. What if we can change the definition of *country*? To bring people together from all around the world? Isn't that at least worth trying?"

That does it.

"I'm in," Mom says. "I vote yes."

"Aye," Dad says. "Let's do it."

. . .

The country's name is the biggest piece of the puzzle, so we start brainstorming right away. We try making up some cool-sounding words, but they all sound like allergy medicines. Looking at the list of names—Zoozaloorakia, Moopoxia—Mom jokes that if Dr. Seuss were alive today, he'd be working in some pharmaceutical company's marketing department, trying to pay off his student loans.

That gets a big laugh out of Dad.

Me and Franny roll our eyes.

"I'm taking five," I say.

I go out to Dad's Dracula production studio, hoping the creative vibes will inspire me. It's spooky and dark, like always. I pace around, thinking. *Come on, come on.*

The name needs to feel *fresh* and *revolutionary* . . . but at the same time kind of *classic* and *timeless*. A bolt of fake lightning strikes, and I see it—this super-cool mythical figure!—back from the dead—just like me in the competition!

Yes! That's it!

I race back inside and yell the name as loud as I can.

WELCOME TO GRANTSYLVANIA
POP. 4

We print up a sign and tape it to the back of Franny's laptop. It's like Transylvania, the home of Dracula, but, you know.

As our newly appointed Ambassador of Arts and Culture, Dad takes it upon himself to design our flag. He does a dramatic reveal in the living room, where he pulls a bedsheet off an easel. Me and Franny and Mom are on the couch. I'm holding my phone up so that Jay—live via video chat—can be a part of the process too.

The flag looks like this:

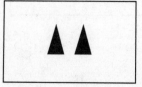

Mom forces a smile. "It's very . . . *creative*," she says.

"Yes!" Dad says, rubbing his hands. "Exactly! That's what I was going for! Something a little abstract, you know? But still clear and strong? It's like—"

"It's two triangles," I say.

"Right, but—"

"Are they supposed to be mountains?" Franny asks.

Mom tilts her head. "Oh yeah! Look! I see it! They're mountains!"

"Why are they mountains?" Jay says. "Aren't you a digital country?"

The vein in Dad's temple is throbbing. It's like the time he attended his own art show in disguise and flipped out because people didn't "get it." He flails in frustration and accidentally knocks the poster board across the room. It hits the wall—*whap!*

We all look over and see it at the same time.

"*Genius,*" I say.

The poster board has flipped upside down. With the two triangles facing downward, they look like . . . Dracula fangs.

"Aw *man*," Franny says. "Good work, Dad. That's perfect!"

24

That afternoon, while Franny's setting up the country's IP address, I jog over to the track. Creating this Internet country is fun and all, and it might just work . . . but I don't want to just *get into* the race. I want to *win* it. And that means I need to outwork all my competitors, push myself to a place they can't reach.

Although, as any runner knows, I have to be smart.

Overtraining leads to injury. I've built a short-term training schedule so I'll be peaking—the best version of myself—when the whole world is watching.

But when I get to the track . . . I'm confused. It's a clear sunny day, and yet, up by the finish line, there's a cluster of black umbrellas.

It reminds me of picture day at school.

And that's when I realize—*a photo shoot.*

"Bro!" Jay says, waving. "Bro! Over here!"

Beside him, a photographer's assistant is tilting a foil-covered board.

"What's this?" I say.

"ESPN. They say I might be the lead story on the website. Crazy, right?"

I can't help it. A blade of jealousy slices through me, followed by disappointment that he hadn't even told me. I mean, he probably just didn't want to hurt my feelings, but our friendship is supposed to be able to be invincible. He should be able to tell me anything.

"This is my best friend," he says to the photographer. "The one I was telling you about. Grant. You should get him in the picture too!"

"Sure," the photographer says, an extremely tall woman with a brown ponytail. "Greg, was it?"

"Grant," I say.

"Right. You know, this is actually perfect. We want to simulate the moment of triumph, what every runner dreams about—crossing the finish line. Having someone to race against will make it feel more natural. You can help us out?"

"Um. Okay."

Me and Jay start walking back toward the starting line.

"That's far enough!" the photographer calls. "Just

need enough to make it look real!" She checks her camera to be sure it's on the correct setting. "Okay, here we go. Ready. Set. *Go!*"

I can't help it. My natural competitiveness takes over. Jay's the same. We fly down the track, crossing the line at what feels like the exact same instant.

"Awesome!" the photographer says, checking the picture display on her camera. "Beautiful! Except . . . George?"

"Grant," I say.

"Right. Listen. Can you slow up just a bit at the end? You know, don't *look like* you're slowing up. If anything, try to look *extra* desperate, like no matter how hard you try, you can't catch him. That's the whole point."

"I don't think I want to do this," I say.

"Oh it's fine!" she says, swapping the lens on her camera for a bigger one. "No one will even notice you! You'll just be an out-of-focus face in the background!"

Jay frowns. "If he doesn't wanna do it, he doesn't wanna do it."

To me he says, "Sorry, bro. I thought it'd be fun."

"It's cool. I'll text you later."

On the way home I stop on the fenced-in bridge over the highway. I grip the rusty fence, staring down at the cars inching along in rush-hour traffic, brake lights flashing red. *I have to make this work,* I think. *I have to get into that race.*

And when I get there, no mercy.

I have to win.

25

That night, using a foam roller on the carpet in Franny's room, I say, "You're going to share our videos with your subscribers, right? To get us started?"

He's weirdly uneasy about this. He tucks his long hair behind his ear and says, tight-mouthed, "Yeah."

We're about to film our first video—our first collaboration in years, the return of G&F Productions. Except our traditional roles have flipped. He's the writer/director. I'm the talent.

"The point here is to build an emotional connection," he says, hanging his green screen on his bedroom wall. "So really open up. I mean, just fully bleed out in front of the camera, explain what this means to you. That's what we need."

"Why do we need the green screen?"

"Because then I can make it look like you're *in* Grantsylvania."

"What does Grantsylvania look like?"

"How should I know? Lots of mountains. Big scary mountains."

Minutes later, I'm magically whisked away to spooky Grantsylvania. Franny puts on headphones and gives me a thumbs-up. *"Action!"*

"Hey, guys!" I say. "My name is—"

"Cut!" Franny yells. "Come on. The 'hey, guys!' thing is so played out. Start again. Just talk from the heart. See if you can make yourself cry. Do you want me to squirt some lemon juice in your eye?"

"No," I say.

"You sure? This is how the sausage is made."

"Just push the stupid button."

He pushes it. *Pling*.

"Hey," I say. "My name is—"

"Cut! Run it again!"

It takes like forty tries to get one usable two-minute take. It makes you wonder how much reality it takes to make one episode of reality TV.

It's a horrible feeling to watch something you've poured your heart into vanish into the cold indifferent void of the Internet.

113

It's pretty clear right away:

No one cares.

The #Grantsylvania hashtag doesn't trend. Even the views for the video are way low by Franny's standard—like two thousand in the first hour.

"I don't get it," I say. "All your other videos are huge. Maybe we shouldn't have made it so sappy."

He's by the window in his room, arms crossed, chewing the inside of his cheek.

"Close the door," he says.

"Huh? Maybe if we—"

"*Close the door.* I don't want Mom and Dad to hear this."

It's weird to see him so frazzled.

"It's all fake," he says.

"What is?"

"My channel. I use a hacker tool to artificially inflate my numbers. The only legit video was *you* at the Penn Relays. That thing blew up. But that was just dumb luck."

Dumb luck? Funny way to think about the worst moment of my life.

Franny stares out the window so he doesn't have to look at me. "You can't come out of nowhere anymore. Not without some serious corporate cash behind you. I'm just like every other invisible kid out there, blabbing into the void. I don't know what else to say. I thought this would catch on. I'm really sorry. You want me to juice the numbers?"

I close my eyes.

Is it really such a big deal? To change a few numbers on the Internet? Who cares? Who would it really hurt? What does it matter *how* I get into the race?

On the other hand . . .

This country is *me*.

Do I really want to cheat? Is that who I am? I feel like if I take a shortcut, I'll regret it forever. "No," I mumble. "Don't do it."

I look again at all the fake awards on Franny's wall. I'm fighting the urge to scream (*How could you do this?*) with the urge to hug him. He's built his whole life around his YouTube channel. To think that all these years he's been spending hours and hours making those videos for . . . no one? Wow. He must be the loneliest kid in the world.

"It's okay," I say. "It was fun while it lasted."

"Grant?" he says.

I turn back, hand on the doorknob. "What?"

"Can you . . . not tell anyone?"

I can actually *see* the shame radiating from him.

He *hates* what he's been doing.

But it's all he has.

"Yeah," I say. "I won't tell anyone. I promise."

"Thanks."

"Good night."

"Good night."

26

I lie awake for hours, mind racing.

It doesn't matter anyway. You would've choked. You'll never be anything. . . .

I get into downward spirals like this where it feels like my brain is spamming itself. I wish there were an option in my preferences that said *To opt out of negative looping thoughts before bed, click here.*

But there isn't.

This is real life.

So what do I do?

I reach for my phone. I need the most boring thing possible—the Internet equivalent of a sleeping pill. The bright light floods my eyes and right away I feel better.

Or rather, I feel *less*. This is our phones' secret, built-in function—they numb us. I search "Babblemoney" and scroll through all the product reviews.

Beneath an avalanche of five-star reviews I find one titled "Is Anyone Reading This?"

> *My uncle works at the factory in Vietnam. He has this tingling in his hands and these dizzy spells. I said maybe the factory's not ventilated? He's breathing in all kinds of dust and stuff? The doctor says no, he just needs rest.*

Sitting up in bed, I bookmark the page.

I scroll and scroll until I'm seasick from it. *Screensick.*

I feel like my bed is spinning.

Finally—exhausted in every way, but still awake—I sneak out of the house and take the only medicine that ever really works for me.

I *run*.

Because it's so late, I run straight down the middle of the street. My reflection jumps along windows of the parked cars. Above, the streetlights cast their shabby orange halos. When I finally get back—sweat drenched—the light is on in Mom's office.

"Little four a.m. jog?" she says, standing by the window, arms crossed. Now that she's done worrying, she's just mad. She's wearing baggy jeans and a blue flannel.

"Sorry," I mutter, head down.

I want to tell her everything. How the Grantsylvania launch was a disaster.

How all this time Franny was basically using Internet steroids to prop up his whole "empire." *But I promised. I promised Franny.* Even in this upside-down family my word has to mean something.

Mom waves me over. I mope across the tiny office and—I can't remember the last time I did this—I fall into her. I totally stop resisting and let her hold me. I'm sweaty from my run, but she doesn't care. She hugs me tight and smells my hair like she must've when I was a newborn. It must be weird to be a parent, to know another human for literally every single second of their life. "Does it still hurt?" she asks, pulling back slightly, squinting.

"Huh?"

"Your chin."

"Oh." When I fell at the Penn Relays, little bits of the track embedded in it. They almost look like little glowing embers. "Nah. I can't even feel them."

"Why don't you get some sleep," she says. "You'll feel better in the morning."

"Okay." I move toward the door. "You stayin' up?"

She smiles tiredly. "Work, work, work."

This is the part of a public defender's life that no one sees. She hates to "go in blind," to speed-read a client's file right before their trial. So she gets up before dawn to review her cases. She could make ten times as much money working for a private law firm. I asked her about it once when we were back-to-school shopping.

"Why would I trade my *time*," she said, pushing the cart, "my *life*, for money?"

"Because we *need* money," I said. "We all do. Or we couldn't buy this school bag. We couldn't buy these pencils. We wouldn't even have a house to live in."

"That's true. And we're lucky. We have enough."

"But wouldn't it be nice to have a *bigger* house?"

"I like our house."

"Come on. You don't fantasize about it?"

"About what?"

"Being rich."

"Of course I do. Don't we all?" She stopped pushing the shopping cart. "You ever stop and wonder why that is, though? Why we all fantasize about it?"

Until that moment I'd never realized that our dreams aren't native to us. They don't just spontaneously appear. They're uploaded from the world around us. Even my own fantasy of breaking the world record had its seed in watching something on TV.

Standing at the bottom of the staircase, foot on the first step, I look over at Mom in her office, half-buried in case files. Her hair is pulled back, deepening the bags beneath her eyes. She sips her coffee and gets to work. This is the race she's chosen.

THE MIDNIGHT SHOW!

Excerpted from ESPN's 30 for 30 documentary, "Crossing the Line: The Incredible True Story of the Million Dollar Race."

Grant Falloon, Track Star

After I talked to Mom that night, I went upstairs and took a long shower. I made it extra hot and was just kind of staring into the steam, lost in my thoughts.

I was remembering that horrible day at the Penn Relays, when I tripped. And as I played it back in my mind, I realized something. I wasn't seeing it through my own eyes. The *video* of the event had overwritten my own memory. I was watching myself from above.

Weird, right?

I got out and dried myself off, still thinking about the video. I grabbed my phone and scrolled back until I found the e-mail I'd gotten from *The Midnight Show! with Jaime Freeman*, back when the meme of me falling was still blowing up. That was, like, seven lifetimes ago in Internet time, but it was worth a shot. . . .

Robert Chum, Intern, *The Midnight Show!*
So yeah. I get this e-mail. From this kid. It was a *reply*—honestly, I'd forgotten I even wrote the first e-mail. [Laughs.] But then I rewatched the video, and, yeah, it all came back. I mentioned it to Jaime in our production meeting, and he was like, "Didn't we have a bit in mind for that?" And I was like, "Yeah, we were gonna do the Second-Chance Time Machine thing, remember?" And he was like, "Ahhhhh! I loved that! Tell the kid to come up here! Let's do it!"

Grant Falloon, Track Star

They wrote back the next morning. They asked if we—our whole family—could come up to New York. I was freaking out. I showed Mom and Dad the e-mail. It took a little convincing, but there we were again, the four of us, back on the Discount Rider bus to New York.

Franny Falloon, Brother

We got there early and were waiting in the greenroom. I thought it was funny that the greenroom was actually painted green.

Dave Falloon, Dad

So we're waiting and one of the show's assistants, this curly-haired woman wearing a headset, came and took us to meet Jaime.

Grant Falloon, Track Star

You have to understand, Jaime Freeman is a *massive* star.

Dave Falloon, Dad

Oh, the kids were over the moon. Soon as they saw him, they floated up and bobbed

on the ceiling like they were balloons.
[Laughs.]

Diane Falloon, Mom
He couldn't have been nicer. He had this
jittery vibe like he'd just drunk six coffees.
Very sweet man. We all went behind his
desk and took a picture.

Grant Falloon, Track Star
I sent the pic to Jay with no explanation.

Jay Fa'atasi, Track Star/Best Friend
I was at the track, training with my brother.
I didn't get it right away. But then I was like,
"Whaaaaaaaaaaaaaaaaat?" I think that was
my actual reply. [Laughs.]

Franny Falloon, Brother
Our segment was prerecorded. Jaime
went to wardrobe and came back wearing
these hilarious gym teacher shorts and a
headband.

Diane Falloon, Mom
They were going to race. . . .

27

At midnight we all gather around Franny's laptop. He puts it on the coffee table and makes it full screen.

"And now, your host, Jaime Freeeeeeeeeman!"

Cramming popcorn in my mouth, I'm both nervous and excited. We left New York right after the segment. We have no idea how they cut it together.

Jaime Freeman emerges through the famous Midnight Show curtain. He smiles. He waves. He clasps his hands. He does his monologue. "We've got a great show for you tonight! Stick around everyone. When we come back, we're debuting a brand-new segment—trust me, you won't want to miss it!"

The crowd cheers.

Cut to commercial.

Dad's pacing behind the couch. "I feel like I'm in a dream. Is this real?"

Jaime Freeman's dancing as the show returns. He acts surprised, like the cameras have just showed up in his living room. "Welcome back! So, I think a common fantasy we all have is that we could go back in time and change the past. Right? We think, oh, I could just go back and say this. Or do that. Then everything would be different. Well, we thought it'd be fun to redo some moments in history . . . but not the ones you'd read about in stuffy history books. Moments like . . . this."

They show the viral video from the Penn Relays.

They slow it down when I trip.

I spill forward, arms wheeling.

My chin skids along the track.

The studio audience goes "Ohhhhhhhhhhhhhhh."

Cut back to Jaime. "Yeah. Ouch. Now let's try that again. Ladies and gentlemen, we present Second-Chance Time Machine!"

Cut to me and Jaime stretching in a corporate-looking hallway. We shake hands and wish each other luck. Way down the hallway, a production assistant yells, "Go!"

Jaime's surprised by how fast I am. You can see it in his eyes.

He never has a chance.

I cross the line—a piece of string held by two interns—and celebrate like I've just set the world record. Jaime jumps around with me. When the segment is over, they cut back to Jaime at his desk. I'm sitting in the plush chair beside him.

"So," he says, "I think we're all wondering, how does it feel to be one of the biggest memes of the year?"

"Well," I say, gripping the arms of the chair tightly. "Not great."

He laughs.

Everyone laughs.

I start to loosen up. "To be honest, I don't even remember it that well," I say. "I guess I just lost concentration for a split second."

"What's going through your mind when you're moving that fast?"

"When I'm at top speed?" I pause to think about it. "It feels like . . . nothing."

"Your head is just totally empty?"

"Yeah."

"Wow. That must be nice. To just . . . disconnect for a few seconds."

"Yeah. It is."

"And are you still racing?"

"Huh?"

"I mean are you still competing?"

"Oh. Yeah. There's actually this huge race this summer. I qualified . . . but they wouldn't let me in."

"Who wouldn't?"

"The race people."

"Why?"

"I didn't have a birth certificate and—"

"Hold on. Wait. I have so many questions. First of all, why don't you have a birth certificate?"

"It's a long story. Basically, my parents aren't big on paperwork. I never got one. I'm sort of a free agent, I guess."

"And because of this you can't race?"

"Yeah."

"Well that stinks."

"I know, right? But then I thought—well, actually this was my brother's idea—he was like, 'If you can't represent America, why not just represent yourself? Why not be your own country?' So I'm actually starting my own country. It's called Grantsylvania. It's a sovereign province of the Internet."

"Wow. And can people like . . . join your country?"

"They can!" I say. "We're going to be putting out new videos every day, so find us on YouTube! Become a citizen!"

"Awesome! Everyone go and check out Grantsylvania! We'll be right back!"

Cut to commercial.

28

Next morning we have seventy-five thousand subscribers, aka citizens. They're pouring in from every part of the world. I want to start making a new video right away, but Franny calls an emergency Family Council in the kitchen. "Sorry," he says. "I know we have a lot to do. But I need to say something. It'll only take a minute."

He turns to Mom and Dad, obviously pained by what he's about to say. "So you know how I've been making my videos for a few years?"

"Of course," Mom says, dumping the water into the coffee maker. "We're so proud. You've built that whole thing up from nothing."

"Well that's the thing," he says. "I kind of . . . *didn't*. I mean, I tried."

Mom looks at Dad, confused.

"You guys probably forget," Franny says, "but for like the first six months my videos got like no views. It didn't matter how hard I worked. I couldn't get any traction. So, what happened was . . . basically, I started juicing my numbers. Just by a little at first. I felt bad about it . . . I really did . . . but then I got addicted. Part of me felt like I was pushing back, fighting for the little guy, like I'd leveled the playing field. But I was still lying, and that's messed up, and I'm sorry. Now that this is blowing up for real, I want everything to be out there, no secrets, total trust."

For a few seconds, the gurgling coffee maker is the only sound in the sunny kitchen.

"You know what really bothers me about all this?" Mom says, leaning back against the counter. "That you even feel that pressure at all. That you have to judge yourself by . . . *views*. What *is* that?"

Franny turns to me. Eyes pleading.

"He's right," I say. "You guys are old. You don't get it."

That addiction he's talking about—I feel it too. In my case it's even more complicated, because, while I have this powerful need to be *liked*, I also hate everyone looking at me.

"*Anyway*," Franny says. "Now that that's out of the

130

way . . . I feel *really* strongly about what we need to do next. You all might not like it at first . . ."

I stop buttering my bagel. *Oh no. What now?*

"But just hear me out. Let's rewind. Go back to the start. What is the point of all this? Why did we even start this country in the first place?"

"To get into the Million Dollar Race," I say.

"Right. Exactly. And how do we do that?"

"We build an online presence so big that Babblemoney sees the PR opportunity and lets me in."

"Or the opposite," Franny says. "That she sees a potential PR *nightmare* coming and lets you in to avoid it, not wanting to be the bad guy. Either way, we need big numbers to make this work. The boost we got from *The Midnight Show!*—it's huge. *But it's not enough.* We have to get to the next level . . . and fast. We only have these eyeballs on us for a *split second*, and we can't let people look away."

"So what's the next step?" Dad asks. "What's the move?"

"Hold on," Franny says. "Give me two minutes. I'll be right back."

29

He comes back holding three things: 1) the GoPro camera he got for his birthday last year, 2) a cheap plastic crown that we used as a prop when we made movies, and 3) a roll of duct tape.

"I don't like this," I say. "I don't know what this is, but I already don't like it."

"Okay," he says, unloading the stuff on the kitchen table. "So here's what I've been thinking about. What *is* Grantsylvania?"

"An Internet country," I say.

"Right. But really, at its heart, it's *you*, right? An online version of you. We could make some videos, tell your story . . . that's what I was originally thinking."

"But . . . ?"

"But the more I think about it, there are zillions of videos like that. People will lose interest. Unless . . . what if we *really* went for it? What if visiting Grantsylvania was like crossing the border into your *actual life*? What if people could look out through your eyes and see what you see? Wouldn't that be the coolest reality TV show of all time?"

Dad's chewing on his lip. "I don't know, son. We could make this country anything. And you want it to be a . . . what? A *videocracy*?"

"Yes! Exactly! This country has one natural resource—Grant. We dig it up and pump it out worldwide, twenty-four seven!"

"How is that even *possible*?" I say.

Franny duct-tapes the GoPro camera to the plastic crown. "This is all you need. It's wireless. The race is in, what, three days? You wear it nonstop until then. We just keep broadcasting around the clock. People can step into your life whenever they want, like tourists."

"Remind me again what this has to do with me getting into the race?" I say.

Franny pinches the bridge of his nose like he's got a brain freeze. "Can't you see? It's all connected. We bring our audience right to Babblemoney's doorstep. You've seen how she acts on camera. If she knows hundreds of thousands of people are watching, we'll have her cornered. It's the perfect trap!"

"Easy for you to say when *I* have to wear that stupid thing," I say. "What if I have to go to the bathroom?"

"We can have commercials. Think about it! This shower is sponsored by Dove Body Wash. This pee is sponsored by Vitaminwater."

"Absolutely not," Mom says. *"No commercials."*

"Fine," Franny says. "Then we play elevator music or something. It's not a big deal. But we can do this. We can start right now! It'll be huge!"

"This is *Grant's* project," Mom says. "The country's got *his* name in it. It's his life." She turns to me, her eyes saying *Anything you decide is fine.*

Man, this is tough. Saying yes will mean doubling down on my trust of Franny. Not only that, but also exposing my weirdo family to the whole world, on purpose.

But it also might give me a real shot at getting back in the race. Which is all that matters, right? I close my eyes like I'm making a wish against my will.

"Okay," I say. "Let's do it. Put that stupid thing on my head."

30

Mom buys plane tickets, and the next morning we all head to the airport. I've got the plastic crown on and am broadcasting live. What I see, the world sees.

I have to take the camera off at airport security, then again on the plane. But during our layover, I strap on the GoPro and run laps around the airport to keep up with my training. The camera bobs on my head as I run.

"Can I just take this thing off?" I say to Franny while I'm doing box jumps on the airport seats. "Is anyone even *watching?*"

He checks the analytics. "Right now? Ninety thousand people."

"For real?"

"I swear."

"*Why?* Is this entertaining?"

He shrugs. "Everybody wonders what it'd be like to be somebody else. It's human nature."

While I run another lap around the concourse, my eye is drawn to the newsstand. I stop and look, chest heaving. It's Jay, flexing on the cover of a magazine.

Above him it says THE NEXT USAIN BOLT? I feel that high-speed collision of feelings inside me again. This time it's pride and jealousy. It makes me dizzy, but I just keep running, fighting through it.

When we finally get to California, we all squeeze into the tiny electric car Dad rented. He grips the steering wheel with both hands and takes a deep, yogalike breath. He hasn't driven in years. The car inches forward, then jerks to a stop.

"Try using just one foot at a time," Mom says. "It's not a bike. You don't pedal it."

"I don't see why I should have to drive like everyone else," Dad says.

Beside me in the back seat, Franny slaps his knee, cracking up. "*Classic.*"

He's watching our show live on his phone.

The car inches forward again, jerks to a stop. The plastic crown digs into my head. Dad flicks on the windshield wipers instead of the flashers.

"This is silly," Mom says. "I'm calling an Uber."

The Uber driver's confused when he pulls up. I guess he doesn't get too many calls from people who are *already in a car*.

Leaning out the driver's-side window, Dad says, "Karl?"

"Yes, sir. You call an U—"

"Karl Behoffer? From the commune? Back in '08?"

The driver squints like he's searching for Dad's younger face beneath his current face. "Ah! Whoa! Dave Falloon! Great to see you, man! How you been?"

"Not bad, not bad. You?"

"Great! I thought you all moved back east?"

"We did. Our son's competing in that youth race up the road."

"The Babblemoney thing?"

"Yeah."

"Cool, man. Heard that's gonna be *wild*. Whole property's been sealed off for weeks."

Dad's smiling with his elbow out the car window. "So you're driving Uber now? What happened to the commune?"

"Eh, was time to move on. Times change, ya know?"

Karl's got a long gray beard and a ponytail. His faded tie-dye shirt is at least twice as old as I am. A happy-looking skeleton is dancing atop the swirling colors. It says GRATEFUL DEAD in psychedelic letters.

I wonder what it means. I'll google it later.

Our motel room has two queen beds. One of them is slanted down and to the left. The curtains are laminated. The NO SMOKING sign has a cigarette burn on it.

"Niiiiiiiice," Dad says, poking his head in the bathroom. "It's an en suite!"

I walk around the room to give our viewers a virtual tour. Weird as it sounds, I'm kind of getting used to the camera. I know that tens of thousands of people are staring at me right now, but from afar the stares are kind of watered down. Or maybe it's the fact that they're not looking *at* me, they're looking *through* me. So in that way I'm sort of an avatar, a vessel for everyone who wants to be on this quest.

G: hey bro. just landed in cali
G: u here yet?

J: bro!
J: flight was delayed
J: take off in a few

G: u wanna meet up
G: where u guys staying

J: babblemoney has these "luxury villas" on her property
J: for the athletes
J: they look pretty sweet

G: nice

J: bro . . .
J: do me a favor
J: look down

G: huh

J: look down at ur phone
J: ah!
J: that's crazy
J: i just sent u a text

J: then i watched u get it

G: ur watching me?
G: right now?

J: dude
J: everyone is watching

Dad orders pizza and salad for dinner. We keep the motel door propped open to air out the stale cigarette smell. "What's the plan tomorrow?" Mom asks, pulling off a slice. "I mean, more specifically?"

"We have to turn up the heat," Franny says, fresh out of the steamy bathroom, twirling a Q-tip in his ear. "Make it so Babblemoney *can't* turn us away, or risk being publicly shamed. I've got an idea."

"Is that something we're comfortable with?" Dad says. "Public shaming?"

"I think if it's a corporation it's okay," Mom says.

"But corporations are *people*," Dad says.

They both laugh for some reason.

Me and Franny roll our eyes.

All playing our roles.

Later, after Mom and Dad have both fallen asleep, I watch *SportsCenter* on mute while Franny patters on his laptop.

I can't imagine that anyone would possibly want to *watch me watching TV*, but the analytics say we still have eighty-seven thousand viewers. Because our audience is global, I guess different countries tune in at different times.

Franny turns his computer screen away from me like he's keeping a secret.

"What are you doing?" I say.

"Research."

"On *what*?"

"Did you know that the Babblemoney Company's weakest performing demographic is youth sales? Age eleven to thirteen?"

"How the heck do you know that?"

"It's all public data. You turn over a few rocks, you never know what might come crawling out."

That reminds me. I search the bookmarks on my phone, looking for the product review that was talking about the Babblemoney factory in Vietnam. The kid who said his uncle was having health problems.

But it's gone.

Like it's been erased.

"Huh," I say. "That's weird."

"What?" Franny says.

Something feels off here—the way you can sense an apple is rotten inside just by holding it, feeling the weight of it.

But is it worth it? To keep digging when I might not

like what I find? Do I want to be stirring up trouble right when I'm about to make my move? *No.* Better to just stay focused on the race. That's what I'm here to do. No distractions.

"Nothing," I say.

The GoPro is uncomfortable, but I roll over, and, after a while, I drift into a shallow, uneasy sleep.

It's the first bit of privacy I've had all day.

Next morning I still have thirty-nine thousand viewers. Even though I've been *sleeping* for the past eight hours. "Creepy," I say out loud. And then—narrating my thoughts for the audience—I say, "I'm going out for a quick run."

It's super foggy outside, and I don't know where I am, so I just jog up the road a mile or so and turn around. "I'm turning around," I say.

When I get back, Dad's sitting on the edge of the motel pool. At first I think he's meditating, but from the way he's slouched, hands under his thighs . . . maybe not.

The thing about the pool is—there's no water in it. He's scissoring his bare feet in a concrete hole. I don't know if he's pretending there's water, or if he's just so lost in his own thoughts he doesn't even notice.

"Hey," I say.

His eyes flick up to the camera on my head, but he doesn't acknowledge it. "Hey." On the lip of the pool, the words "no diving" have faded to O IVIN.

I sit beside him. Without water, the pool ladders look ridiculous, like they're clinging to the edge of a cliff.

"Would've been your grandfather's sixtieth birthday today," he says.

"Really? Grandpa Falloon?"

"Yeah. I was thinking how much he would've loved to be here. To see you race. He was a star football player. A wide receiver. I ever tell you that? He broke the school record for catches his senior year. He could fly."

"So maybe I get it from him," I say.

It's tempting to imagine yourself like a genetic pie chart—60 percent Mom's side, 40 percent Dad's—though I know the math is way more complicated.

Dad plucks a frill off his self-cut jean shorts. He rubs it into a ball and flicks it into the empty pool. "Yeah. Maybe."

"What was he like?" I ask.

"He was . . . quiet. He was always so tired after work. We'd sit down to dinner, and the house would just be totally silent. Mom had been dead a long time. It was just the two of us. Honestly, that's what I remember most—the sound of our forks scraping on our plates."

"He was a painter, right?"

"Yeah. This guy, Mr. Sheffield, he had a big painting company in town. Your grandfather started working summers in high school, same job his whole life."

I think of those cars inching along in morning traffic. "That was what he wanted to do? That was his dream?"

"I don't think his generation thought of work that way."

"He didn't go to college?"

"No. Well, actually—he did for a few weeks. But football didn't work out and he left. After he died, I found his old class schedule in the attic. He'd kept it—I don't know why. Maybe like he would go back someday. He always loved to read. He would leave me the *Daily News* before school, opened to the football standings, trying to get me interested, but I don't know—it just never stuck. I guess maybe it skips a generation."

A car pulls into the motel parking lot, headlights cutting through the fog.

"You know the last thing I ever said to him?" Dad says, crossing his ankles in the empty pool. "Before your Mom and I moved to California? One word. I said, '*Fine.*'"

"What did he say?"

"He said"—Dad's lip quivers—"'Then don't ever come back here again.'"

Thinking about Grandpa Falloon, I realize why Dad comes to all my track meets even though he doesn't like sports. Why we have to say what we're feeling before we eat dinner. He can't fix what happened with his dad, but he can pay it forward to me.

I think it's probably like that in every family, this relay race where the parent keeps dropping the baton, and the kid keeps picking it up, racing like mad to make up for lost ground, but then *he* drops it when he's giving it to *his* kid, because he's overcompensating, and so on, forever and ever.

We sit side by side, legs dangling in the empty pool.

Finally I say, "I'm sorry, Dad."

"For what?"

"For everything. I've kind of been in a funk for a while. I guess I've been taking it out on you guys."

"It's okay, son. That's how this story always goes." He stands and offers me his hand. "Now come on. Let's go win that million bucks."

33

"Okay," Franny says, pacing in the motel room. He's drawn an incredibly detailed map of the Babblemoney estate on our pizza box from last night. "The plan is to stage a protest outside gate A—*here*."

"Protest?" I say.

"Trust me," he says. "If there's one thing the Internet can't get enough of, it's kids protesting stuff. This thing is gonna blow up."

We Uber over and begin marching in circles outside Babblemoney's castlelike walls ("NO NATIONS LEFT BEHIND! NO NATIONS LEFT BEHIND!"). Franny e-mail blasts our now two-hundred-thousand-plus citizens—for those who aren't already watching—and the viewers start rising quickly.

My brother was born for this. The fake outrage oozes out of him so naturally. "My brother *deserves* to be here," he says. "Our nation *demands* to be recognized. . . . If you're out there watching, Babblemoney, I want you to look closely!"

He holds up my birth certificate printed on official Republic of Grantsylvania letterhead. "We've got the paperwork!"

There's a harsh buzzing sound, and the gate scrapes open behind us. I turn, half expecting trumpets to blare and horses to thunder out. But it's just an electric golf cart. It's one of those long ones with a flashing yellow light that can hold like ten people. The driver is wearing sunglasses and a coiled earpiece. "Grant Falloon?" he says.

I cross my arms. "Yeah?"

"We're gonna need you to shut down this protest."

"No can do," I say.

"Ms. Babblemoney would like to have a word with you."

"Oh would she now?"

"Yes. Please come with me."

"That's my *son* you're talking to," Dad says with an edge in his voice I've never heard before. "He's not going anywhere without me. Without all of us."

We all link arms and stand together in front of the gate. The guard sighs. "They told me you people were—" He notices the camera on my head and stops himself from whatever he was going to say.

We climb into the extra-long golf cart. You can tell Babblemoney is super rich, because after almost ten minutes of driving—on her property the whole time—we're still not there. In the distance we see cranes and hear beeping trucks.

The guard leads us into what looks like the world's largest Foot Locker. It's a *sneaker museum*, all the Babblemoney sneaker models displayed on the walls. There must be five thousand of them, all the way up to the ceiling on both sides.

On the far wall is a massive oil painting of Ms. Babblemoney in her red tracksuit and pearls. Beside that is a world map showing all 917 of their outlet stores, each marked with the dollar-sign B. The old woman is waiting on her red scooter.

"Greetings," I say as formally as I can, adjusting my camera crown to center her in the shot. "We come from the sovereign Republic of Grantsylvania."

Mom unfurls our wrinkled flag—the two triangles upside down that look like Dracula fangs.

Babblemoney looks like she wants to spit but can't because her mouth is too dry. "Can't say I'm happy to see *you lot* again," she says.

"Yeah," I say. "Well, we're Falloons. We don't give up that easily."

Babblemoney notices the GoPro on my head.

One of her guards whispers something in her ear.

And it's amazing: In less than a second she transforms into the sweet, smiling old grandma. "So," she says warmly. "I hear you have a new . . . territory."

"Yeah," I say. "You're lookin' at it."

"Excuse me?"

"I'm the country."

"Forgive me . . . I don't understand."

"It's just a version of me that's on the Internet. I have citizens that subscribe to my life." I peek down at my phone. "Right now, in case you were wondering, we have four hundred fifty thousand viewers. You can wave to them if you like."

Franny nudges me like *no more messing around.*

"We've come a really long way," I say. "All we're asking is that you open your mind to what a country can *be.* All we're asking is—"

"Do you know why I started this competition?" Babblemoney asks, gazing down at her fingernails like she hasn't even been listening.

"Because you've got more dough than you know what to do with?"

She smirks. "I do. But that's not the reason. No, I created this competition because I wanted to *inspire*. Do you know what my father said to me on my sixteenth birthday? When I told him I planned to go to college to study economics?"

I shrug.

"He said, 'Go on and waste your time if you want.' He didn't see any point in a *girl* educating herself. That was the world *I* grew up in. And so you know what I did? The day I graduated, I started my own company. A sneaker company. And I put his out of business."

"Must've felt nice," Franny says.

"It *did*," Babblemoney says. "I've enjoyed it all *thoroughly*."

"No," Franny says. "I mean to have gone to college when it cost like four cents."

She ignores him. She's in full Grandma Mode now.

"Yes, my intention here, from the start, has been to *inspire*. And I must say . . . I didn't expect this. I didn't expect to be *inspired myself*. What you've done here, young man, is remarkable. I know what it takes to build something from scratch, against the odds. I respect that. And so you know what? I'm making an exception. I say welcome, Grant Falloon of Grantsylvania. You may compete in my race . . . though of course, as a visitor, you must obey the local laws and customs."

"Laws?" I say. "Customs?"

"Well, to start, you'll need to remove that crown. There are others here who have paid a great price for what we here call the 'broadcasting rights.' We must respect that, don't you think?"

One of her beefy, short-armed security guards steps forward. When he talks, he sounds like he just swallowed his own Adam's apple. "I'll take that."

I have to say, as I lift the crown off my head, I do feel suddenly less powerful.

We're escorted out of the room by security. Last I see of Babblemoney, she's parked beneath that epic wall of sneakers, watching us go, sucking on her dentures.

Or maybe she's just smirking. It's hard to tell.

34

There's a big welcome party that night. Within a few hours, Babblemoney's sneaker museum has been transformed into a ritzy-looking ballroom. The soft purple lighting reminds me of those UV lights used to whiten teeth.

"Who *are* all these people?" I mutter to Franny.

He frowns. "Bigwigs from all the sponsoring companies."

A few feet away, a man in an expensive suit is pointing at me. He sips his cocktail and says something to his friend. The friend laughs.

I've just taken two meat-on-a-sticks from a passing server (they're delicious, dripping with fat) when I spot Jay and his family. He's wearing a red polo shirt, blue shorts, and white flip-flops. His sunglasses are on top of his head.

"Bro!" he says. "What happened to the show? Babble-money canceled you?"

I laugh. "Yeah. I guess she kind of did."

"You do remember that I had that idea first, right? For the show?"

"You did?"

"Are you kidding? I *begged* you!"

"Yeah, well, not everything has to be a competition."

He looks at me like an alien is inhabiting my body.

"Sorry," I say. "Of course it does. You're right. You had the idea first."

We laugh, and for a split second, despite the fact that we're in this swanky ballroom, it feels like we're back home in the neighborhood.

"Be honest," I say. "Was a little part of you—even the tiniest little part—hoping that Babblemoney wouldn't let me in the race?"

"Yeah," he admits. "But only because I know you can beat me. But then I realized it's better that way. I won't have to always wonder if I'm the best. One way or another, I'll know." He extends his fist. "No mercy."

"No hard feelings," I say.

We fist-bump.

He leaves to eat with his family, and I can't really get comfortable the rest of the night. I stare down at my feet, feeling like a machine that's been improperly assembled.

It makes me wonder if I'll *ever* be comfortable in my own skin, or if this is just the curse of being human. We can evolve as much as we want, build skyscrapers and space stations and stuff, dress up and wear fancy clothes . . . but deep down we'll always just be these insecure apes, looking around at the other apes, wondering *Do they like me?*

THE MILLION DOLLAR RACE

PRELIMS

Excerpted from ESPN's 30 for 30 documentary, "Crossing the Line: The Incredible True Story of the Million Dollar Race."

Leonard Lish, Emmy-Winning TV Producer
The way the Babblemoney people had it
set up originally, they were just going to
run prelims and then have a final race, like
they'd done at regionals and nationals. I
said, "Why not mix it up a little?"
I pitched it as a two-day event. Day one
you introduce all the characters, get
everyone emotionally invested. Day two,
instead of just a final race, you have a

single elimination tournament—a final
four. I said, "It's like the Kentucky Derby
meets March Madness." The old lady
loved that.

Jay Fa'atasi, USA

The corporate tents were endless. I
couldn't even count them all.

Diane Falloon, Mom

There was a corner of the estate used for
parking private jets. [Shakes head.]

Jay Fa'atasi, USA

We all got our own "luxury villas" with our
country's flag flying outside.

Grant Falloon, Grantsylvania

The opening ceremony was Saturday
morning. Babblemoney was up on this
platform in her red tracksuit and pearls,
holding a wireless microphone. I couldn't
figure out what she was waiting for. Then
I saw the producer beside her. He had his
hand up, giving the HOLD sign. He was
waiting for word from the TV truck that
they were back from commercial.

Leonard Lish, Emmy-Winning TV Producer
Maybe you've never thought of sports as a kind of reality TV show. But that's exactly what they are. Look closer next time you go to a game. Professional arenas are just big, expensive TV studios.

Grant Falloon, Grantsylvania
They didn't even build a whole track for the races. It was just the straightaway, the hundred meters, surrounded on all sides by TV towers.

Jay Fa'atasi, USA
I mean, I want to say it was weird being surrounded by all those cameras . . . but to be honest, it wasn't that different from a normal day at school. Someone is always filming something. [Laughs.]

Grant Falloon, Grantsylvania
Yeah, but there were also dance teams and corporate mascots and rich people wandering around in big funny hats.

Jay Fa'atasi, USA
True, true. Makes you realize how crazy life

159

must be for professional athletes. There's all this noise, and you're just . . . doing your job. You're at work. That was how I looked at it. I was all business. I was leaving with that million bucks.

Franny Falloon, Brother
The boys' prelims were first.

Leonard Lish, Emmy-Winning TV Producer
There's a natural hierarchy in track—the sprinters are at the top. They're the celebrities; the track is their red carpet. But even within that top level there are tiers. And of this group, the American Fa'atasi, was at the top, the A-lister. Falloon was a curiosity, because of the Internet thing, but he was kind of awkward.

Grant Falloon, Grantsylvania
Since winning at nationals, Jay had become a star. A camera crew was following his every move.

Franny Falloon, Brother
Jay was in the first heat.

Grant Falloon, Grantsylvania

He was so fast. He looked like he was
moving at one and a half times normal
speed. He won his heat *easily*. I felt like
one of us was definitely going to break the
record.

Jay Fa'atasi, USA

The record was still 10.73. I ran a 10.75. So
close.

Grant Falloon, Grantsylvania

The kid from Jamaica ran a 10.78.
The Japanese kid ran a 10.79.
There was a big group all bunched at 10.80.
That meant I had to run a 10.79 to make the
final four.

Dave Falloon, Dad

I just didn't want him to trip. *Anything* but
that. Just cross the line.

Dan Rossum, Broadcaster

[Transcript from TV]
Okay, folks, welcome back! Here we are,
the final boys' heat of day one. Russia in

lane one. China in lane two. New Zealand in
lane three. France in lane four. Peru in lane
five. Zimbabwe in lane six. Greece in lane
seven. And there in lane eight—the young
man everyone has been talking about—
representing himself—Grant Falloon from
Grantsylvania.

Jay Fa'atasi, USA
Grant and the kid from Peru jumped out
in front. They were even for a while. But
Grant was faster. He pulled ahead.

Dan Rossum, Broadcaster
[Transcript from TV]
Falloon takes it! And goodness, Rebecca—
look at that time.

Rebecca Moffet, Color Commentator
[Transcript from TV]
Wow—10.76! Just shy of Fa'atasi! Oh, what a
final four this is going to be!

35

That night I'm with my family in our "luxury villa." Unlike the motel, everything in it is gleaming and spotless and futuristic-looking. From the helicopters circling above, the villas probably look like rows of futuristic space pods.

Mom and Dad are shoulder to shoulder in bed, reading the same book. (Because they're corny like that.) I open the minifridge to get a bottle of water . . . and the handle breaks off. For a few seconds I'm just standing there, holding it, confused.

"What a piece of junk," I say.

"Figures," Franny says. "This is all just for show. It's like that fake music festival a few years ago. This room just needs to look good in a *picture*."

"I'm taking a walk," I say. "I can't breathe in here."

Outside, the night sky is so crowded with stars I almost wonder if Babblemoney had them CGI'd into the sky. She's so rich, anything seems possible.

I walk down the row of "luxury villas," lost in my own thoughts. Next thing I know I'm at the track. Without fans or broadcasters, it really does just look like a desolate TV studio.

I kneel in the starting blocks and press my fingertips into the spongy-hard track. I drop my head. I lift my hips. I close my eyes and inhale deeply, feeling the cool night air tracing the outline of my body. I simulate my start, and that's when I notice someone else down at the far end of the track. They're in lane one, stepping foot over foot like they're on a tightrope. I'd know that posture anywhere—*it's Jay*. He's wearing a red-white-and-blue tracksuit and big noise-canceling headphones.

"Hey!" I call, dropping my voice lower so I sound like a security guard. "You're not supposed to be here!"

He spins, startled.

I smirk.

He pulls off one side of his headphones. "*You're* the one who's not supposed to be here," he shoots back. And I have to give it to him: It's true.

We walk toward each other.

"What you doing out here?" I ask.

"Well I *was* measuring this track—"

"With your *feet*?"

"I didn't bring a tape measure, bro. But I looked it up. A hundred meters is three hundred and twenty-eight feet, give or take a few inches. So . . ."

I know what he's thinking: *If I'm gonna break the record, I want this track to be official, not a foot too short or too long.* I know he's thinking it, because I'm thinking it.

Just then a voice calls from behind us. "Hey! You're not supposed to be here!"

We both spin, startled.

But it's just Franny. He steps out of the shadows, onto the track, grinning like *gotcha.* Jay shakes his head, frowning. "The Falloon sense of humor must be genetic."

"Guys," Franny says, reaching into his pocket. "Listen. I know you're trying to focus on your race. But you both need to know something. *I figured it out.*"

"Figured out *what*?" I say.

"What this is all about. I did some snooping while the races were happening. Look at *this.*" He shows us a picture of what appears to be a warehouse full of boxes.

"Wow," Jay says. "She's got . . . boxes. Let's call the cops."

"Boxes of *these.*" Franny points down at his feet. I can't believe I hadn't noticed. He's wearing these shiny, futuristic-looking sneakers. At first glance they appear to be made of tinfoil.

"They're amazingly light," he says, shifting his weight on the track. "I can barely feel them on my feet at all. I could probably dust you both right now."

Me and Jay look at each other . . . and bust out laughing.

"Wait," I say, my laugh trailing off. "You *stole* those?"

"Think about it," Franny says. "You've got a brand-new product you want to unveil. The hottest thing since Crocs or those stupid toe sneaker things."

"I like those," I say.

"You would. But stay with me. You want to launch a new product in a crowded marketplace. What's the best way to do it?"

"Um, make a commercial?"

"Can't you *see*?" Franny pinches the bridge of his nose like we—the two track stars—are unbearably slow. "It's like I've been saying from the beginning. This whole thing *is* the commercial. They've built this whole 'experience' to sell these stupid"—he points at his feet—"*whatever* they are."

I pace with my hands on my head. "*Franny*. We can't be thinking about this right now. We have the biggest race of our lives tomorrow. It's for a million bucks."

Franny looks around at the world-class outdoor TV studio. "Drop in the bucket," he says.

"Huh?"

"A million bucks. Drop in the bucket of an advertising budget for a company like Babblemoney's. It's not a prize.

It's an *investment*. How much you wanna bet you'll be racing in *these* tomorrow?"

He's snapping pictures of the futuristic sneakers from all angles.

"So what?" I say. "Even if everything you say is true . . . so what? How's it any different from the Olympics? Or the Super Bowl? It's all just one big commercial with some sports in between. We still get to race with the whole world watching. One of us still gets the million bucks. That's all that matters." I turn to Jay. "Right?"

Jay nods, but he's squinting like he's still processing what Franny is telling us. Franny peeks over his shoulder to be sure no one's listening.

"Wait," he says. "There's more."

36

"So you know how we have that Contact Us page on the Grantsylvania site?" he says.

"We do?" I say.

"Yeah. It's kind of buried. To be honest I just put it on there 'cuz Dad made me. I didn't think people would actually *use* it. But they are. We have thousands of messages. I started responding and—hold on, I'll show you."

He opens a video chat app on his phone. Seconds later a dark-haired boy our age appears on the screen. I can't figure out why the kid's so excited at first—wide-eyed, open-mouthed. Then I realize. He's *starstruck*. "Grant!" he says. "Is it really you?"

I wave awkwardly. "Hey."

"Ah! And is that Jay?"

Jay flashes a peace sign. "What up?"

"This is Hilmi," Franny says. "He's from Malaysia. Hold on." He patches in another boy from China, Xu, and a girl from India, Saanjh.

We're all on the same video chat.

The kids take turns telling their stories. "A stitching machine exploded," Saanjh says. "My grandpa was burned. The factory is still open."

"My mom's arm was crushed," says Xu.

"The company covered it up," Hilmi says. "A man came to give us money, but Mom won't take it. She says it's *blood* money. We don't know what to do. No one will listen. They've paid off the mayor and the newspapers and the TV stations, even the doctors."

"Do you have evidence?" Franny asks. "Pictures? Videos?"

"Of course," Hilmi says. "But I'm telling you—*no one cares*. It's impossible. There's nothing we can do."

Listening to their stories, I can't help thinking how I would feel if Mom's arm got crushed, or if Dad's hands went numb and he couldn't make art anymore . . . if they could potentially *die* just because they're trying to provide for their family. It sounds so insane—but to these kids it's real. We just don't hear about it.

If I'm honest, there's a part of me that wishes I *didn't* know. That I could just go on like before. Chasing my dream without the weight of knowing.

I look over at Jay. Three months ago we were just two kids from East Falls dreaming of fortune and glory.

Three *minutes* ago we were just two kids caught up in a sneaker company's marketing scheme.

But now it feels like everything's changed. If we go through with the race—if we keep our mouths shut because we want the money—we're no better than everyone else Babblemoney has paid off along the way. We're *accomplices.*

And yet . . . what can we do? What power do we—a bunch of kids—really have?

"Maybe we should just tell everyone now," I say. "We blast it out to our citizens with some pictures and—"

"Yeah," Jay says, "but if we tell everyone *now*, the whole race might get called off, right?"

"So?" I say.

"So think about it. What happens? It causes a little stir for like a *day* . . . it trends for like twenty minutes . . . and then everyone forgets. . . ."

"But Babblemoney *doesn't*," I say, finishing his thought, "and with all her connections we get blacklisted and never get another sponsorship ever again."

"Not to mention her factories go right back to doing what they were doing," Franny says.

"But there *has* to be a way," I say.

Frustrated, I tip my head back and stare up at the constellation of TV cameras. I imagine all the other kids lining the track for the final races. I imagine Babblemoney in her red tracksuit, waving to the crowd. A plan starts to form in my head. I smirk.

"Or what if . . ."

GIRLS' FINAL FOUR

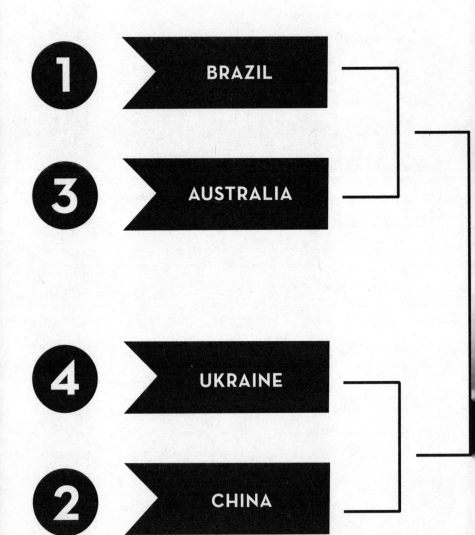

BOYS' FINAL FOUR

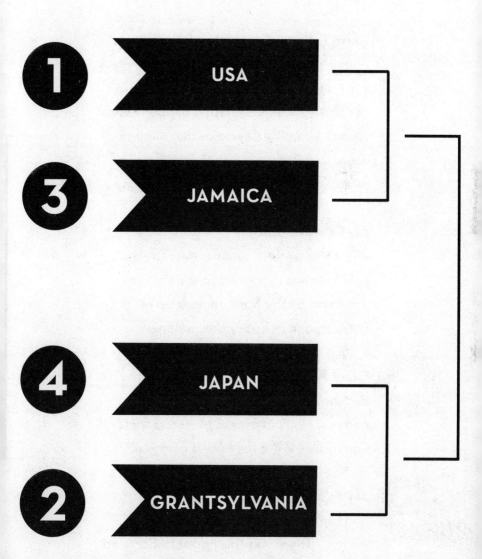

Excerpted from ESPN's 30 for 30 documentary, "Crossing the Line: The Incredible True Story of the Million Dollar Race."

Grant Falloon, Grantsylvania

All the kids who'd already been eliminated stayed to watch the finals. This wasn't like the NBA championship that happens every year, or even the Olympics that happen every four. This was a *once-in-a-lifetime* event.

Jay Fa'atasi, USA

It was this perfect summer day. The girls' final four was supposed to start at ten a.m. I was by the track, looking up at Babblemoney's luxury box, waiting. . . .

Grant Falloon, Grantsylvania

But she wasn't up there. I started getting nervous. I looked over at Mom and Dad and Franny like, *What the heck is going on?*

Jay Fa'atasi, USA

Suddenly this shadow passed over us— *whoosh!* There was this huge blast of wind. We all looked up—

Grant Falloon, Grantsylvania

A helicopter. A black helicopter with the Babblemoney *B* painted on it. The *B* with the dollar sign through it.

Jay Fa'atasi, USA

Babblemoney was arriving in style. It was like her property was so big she had to take a helicopter from one end to the other. [Laughs.]

Grant Falloon, Grantsylvania

The helicopter landed on the end of the track, about twenty yards past the finish line. She came down the ramp in her electric scooter, waving like a queen. Of course wearing her red tracksuit and her pearls.

Jay Fa'atasi, USA

All these security guards started pouring out of the helicopter like commandos. They were carrying black briefcases, looking super serious.

Grant Falloon, Grantsylvania

They opened the suitcases and set them on what looked like Olympic medal stands.

Jay Fa'atasi, USA
My eyes almost popped out of my head.

Diane Falloon, Mom
They were filled with *cash*.

Esther Babblemoney, Sneaker Queen
[Transcript from TV broadcast]
Welcome to the final day of the Million
Dollar Race! Behind me, in the cases
guarded by these nice gentlemen, are *two
million dollars*, one for our girls' champion,
one for our boys'! The *instant* the winners
are decided, you will be immediately flown
in my private helicopter to the nearest
bank, where you will deposit the money in
a trust fund created in your name!

Leonard Lish, Emmy-Winning TV Producer
No one had seen anything like this before.
That was the point.

Grant Falloon, Grantsylvania
It almost felt like a game show.

Jay Fa'atasi, USA
Or a WWE match or something.

Leonard Lish, Emmy-Winning TV Producer

Babblemoney was always an advertising genius. Even at age ninety or whatever she was, she still had it.

Sefina Fa'atasi, Jay's Mom

She said some boring stuff; then she was like—

Esther Babblemoney, Sneaker Queen

[Transcript from TV broadcast]
[Looks right at camera.]
And that is why we wanted to bring the whole world together for this competition. We like to imagine that, in the years to come, as we humans push ever outward, there will be not only global competitions, but *intergalactic* games. With an eye on that dazzling future, we are proud to introduce the ZeroGravity3000s!

Grant Falloon, Grantsylvania

They brought out the silver sneakers.

Jay Fa'atasi, USA

It was funny. It looked like they were displaying a product on *The Price Is Right*.

I started hearing that music in my head.
Da-dunt-da-da, da-dunt-da-da.

Franny Falloon, Brother
I mouthed to Grant, *Told you!*

Esther Babblemoney, Sneaker Queen
[Transcript from TV broadcast]
[Smiling.] That's right. Every pair of ZG3s is
custom-fitted using our revolutionary new
Scan Your Foot app™. Every pair will fit you,
the runner, perfectly! You'll feel like you're
racing on the moon!™

Dave Falloon, Dad
Their app was available on Apple and
Android platforms the same day. There
were one and a half million downloads the
first hour.

Grant Falloon, Grantsylvania
The camera people were following the girls
around, filming their feet.

Franny Falloon, Brother
While everyone was distracted, Jay's
brother and I had a secret mission. He was

my lookout. I ducked under a rope and army crawled toward the TV truck.

Tua Fa'atasi, Jay's Brother
I was like, "Bro, what are you doing?"

Franny Falloon, Brother
I guess I didn't really have to army crawl. I stood up and did my thing with the wires.

Tua Fa'atasi, Jay's Brother
At one point this security guard came over to see what was going on. I blocked him and pretended like I was lost until Franny got out of there.

Franny Falloon, Brother
Mission accomplished.

Grant Falloon, Grantsylvania
Me and Jay watched the girls' races from the side of the track. The girls looked over and nodded before the race, and we nodded back.

Adriana Santos, Brazil
Grant and Jay had come to us early in the morning, before the broadcast started.

Grant Falloon, Grantsylvania
We told all the other athletes at breakfast. Real quiet, holding our phones low so we could show them the pictures and the videos from the factories.

Jay Fa'atasi, USA
The videos spoke for themselves. But we also had a translator app, because a lot of the kids didn't speak English. We probably couldn't have done it twenty years ago.

Maggie Olinyk, Ukraine
They told us everything. How workers had been hurt making the shoes that we'd be helping to sell.

Adriana Santos, Brazil
At first we were just in shock.

Maggie Olinyk, Ukraine
It's like all these emotions hit you at the same time. You're mad at what you've just seen, but you're also afraid, and disappointed, and another part of your brain is saying, *Well it's not like you're going to be able to change anything anyway.*

Adriana Santos, Brazil

And then comes this moment of truth. You
have all the facts, and you have to decide:
Okay, what am I going to do?

Grant Falloon, Grantsylvania

We didn't want to pressure anyone into
anything. We knew how much everyone
had invested in the race, both the time
they'd already spent training and what it
could mean for the future.

Jay Fa'atasi, USA

We just said, "Look. Here's what's up.
Here's what we're thinking. If you want in,
awesome. If not, we totally understand."

Franny Falloon, Brother

The races went off as scheduled.

Grant Falloon, Grantsylvania

The Brazilian girl beat the Ukrainian girl in
the first race.

Jay Fa'atasi, USA

The Australian girl beat the Chinese girl in
the second.

Jay Fa'atasi, USA

The Brazilian girl won the final. She was jumping around with her family . . . and that was real, man. Real joy. She had worked really hard for that moment. I honestly had a tear in my eye.

Franny Falloon, Brother

And then it was just like Babblemoney had said. The girl was whisked off in the helicopter with the money.

Grant Falloon, Grantsylvania

I have to admit, seeing that . . . I started having second thoughts. I started daydreaming about that mansion with all the flat-screen TVs and the sneaker-shaped pool.

Jay Fa'atasi, USA

I elbowed him and told him to stay focused.

Diane Falloon, Mom

The closer it got to the boys' races, the more nervous I got. Babblemoney was up in her luxury box, waving to the crowd, the belle of the ball. I thought, *Just you wait.* . . .

Franny Falloon, Brother

Yeah. We'd told our parents. It's always risky turning information over to the adult world—you never know what they might do with it. But we felt like we had to. We'd come so far. We were all in this together.

Dave Falloon, Dad

When they told us, I wanted to call the cops right away. But the boys convinced me there was a better way. A way to use the spectacle of the race to our advantage.

Jay Fa'atasi, USA

The helicopter came back and landed at the end of the track. The money started blowing out of the briefcases. It was funny watching the guards chase after it. [Laughs.]

Dan Rossum, Broadcaster

[Transcript from TV broadcast]
Okay, folks, here we go! Looks like they've got the track cleaned up, and we're almost ready for our next semifinal! Very soon one of these four boys will be flying off to a whole new life. First up, it's Japan versus Grantsylvania!

Natsu Watanabe, Japan

It's true, yes, Grant and Jay talked to us
that morning. But they never asked us to
lose. I feel that is important to say. We were
all trying to win.

Dan Rossum, Broadcaster

[Transcript from TV broadcast]
There they are, folks, Falloon and Watanabe.
Just a fraction of a second separates these
boys. Buckle up. Anything could happen.

Natsu Watanabe, Japan

They filmed us lacing up the new
Babblemoney sneakers.

Grant Falloon, Grantsylvania

I was rolling my neck just before the race.
I peeked over at my family. I didn't say
anything. But I nodded. They nodded back.

Dan Rossum, Broadcaster

[Transcript from TV broadcast]
Okay, looks like the boys are all laced
up and ready to go. Ms. Babblemoney
watching from her box. Here we go. Falloon
and Watanabe.

Rebecca Moffet, Color Commentator

[Transcript from TV broadcast]

I'm nervous, Dan, and I'm not even racing!
Here we go.

Dan Rossum, Broadcaster

[Transcript from TV broadcast]

And they're off! A clean start for both
runners!

Rebecca Moffet, Color Commentator

[Transcript from TV broadcast]

They're neck and neck! Thirty meters. Fifty
meters. Seventy meters.

Dan Rossum, Broadcaster

[Transcript from TV broadcast]

Falloon pulls ahead, now Watanabe,
now Falloon! Here's the finish—oh it's
close!

Rebecca Moffet, Color Commentator

[Transcript from TV broadcast]

Falloon! Falloon takes it by a step!

Grant Falloon, Grantsylvania

Just short of the record again. 10.74.

Dan Rossum, Broadcaster

[Transcript from TV broadcast]

Okay, Falloon is through to the final. But who will he face?

Rebecca Moffet, Color Commentator

[Transcript from TV broadcast]

It's the American versus the Jamaican in our next semifinal. No secret who the crowd here in California is pulling for.

Devon Jones, Jamaica

Yeah, man, the crowd was definitely against me. [Laughs.] They were chanting "U-S-A! U-S-A!" It was really loud. There was only this one lady who was chanting—

Diane Falloon, Mom

Everyone do your best! Everyone do your best!

Grant Falloon, Grantsylvania

[Laughs.] Mom was doing her thing. I stayed by the finish line to watch. Jay made the sign of the cross and pointed to the sky. He looked ready.

Dan Rossum, Broadcaster

[Transcript from TV broadcast]

Here we go. The American and the
Jamaican. The winner is through to the final.
The runners take their places. They drop
their heads. They're set. And . . . they're off!
The Jamaican takes the early lead! He's out
in front! He's flying down the track! But now
here comes Fa'atasi! He's gaining ground!

Jay Fa'atasi, USA
They had this giant HD screen at the end
of the track. It was weird because, while
you were racing, you could look straight
ahead and . . . watch yourself racing. It was
like how a football player can look up and
watch himself on the Jumbotron as he's
crossing into the end zone.

Grant Falloon, Grantsylvania
The finish was too close to call. They were
replaying it on the HD screen in super slo-mo.
The crowd gasped when they stopped it. I had
to laugh.

Jay Fa'atasi, USA
I *swear* I didn't mean to do it. But
there I was, leaning over the line like a
lowercase *r* . . .

Grant Falloon, Grantsylvania
He stole my move! [Laughs.]

Leonard Lish, Emmy-Winning TV Producer
That set up the final everyone was hoping
for. The American vs. the Grantsylvanian.
For Babblemoney it was perfect, her two
brightest stars.

Jay Fa'atasi, USA
Babblemoney had come down onto the
track.

Franny Falloon, Brother
She was on her scooter, just past the finish
line, surrounded by her flex of security
guards.

Grant Falloon, Grantsylvania
Just before the race, Franny and Tua
flashed thumbs-ups.

Dan Rossum, Broadcaster
[Transcript from TV broadcast]
Okay, folks! No more messing around! This
is it! The Million Dollar Race!

Rebecca Moffet, Color Commentator
[Transcript from TV broadcast]
Look at that, Dan. The stakes are so high
Falloon and Fa'atasi won't even look at each
other. Intense!

Dan Rossum, Broadcaster
[Transcript from TV broadcast]
Both of them glaring down the track, eyes
literally on the prize.

Grant Falloon, Grantsylvania
Right before the race started, when we
were down in the starting blocks, I reached
out my fist.

Jay Fa'atasi, USA
I did the same.

Grant Falloon, Grantsylvania
We met in the middle.

Jay Fa'atasi, USA
A no-look fist bump.

Grant Falloon, Grantsylvania

I have this routine I do before every race. I
imagine that my mind is a computer screen.
All my thoughts are like files on the desktop.
I saw Dad in his art studio. I saw Mom in
her office late at night. I saw me and Franny
making movies in our backyard. I saw Jay and
Tua and Mrs. Fa'atasi at her party. It was like
when you flick your phone with your thumb
and your timeline flies by, you know?
And then everything went dark.
I was ready.

Rebecca Moffet, Color Commentator

[Transcript from TV broadcast]
Something slightly different here, Dan. Ms.
Babblemoney is going to count down for the final.

Esther Babblemoney, Sneaker Queen

[Transcript from TV broadcast]
Runners on your marks . . .
Get set . . .
Go!

Dan Rossum, Broadcaster

[Transcript from TV broadcast]
Wow! Look at that! *Great* start for Falloon!

Grant Falloon, Grantsylvania

I had the early lead. I had him by a half step. But I could feel him on my hip, pushing me. I kept my eyes forward. I wasn't going to make that mistake again, like at the Penn Relays, lose concentration.

Louis Carlssen, Renowned Track Coach

Most people think that a sprint is constant acceleration, that you just keep building speed until the end. But that's not true.

About a third of the way in, you've already reached your top speed. That "final burst" you see on TV, it's an optical illusion, one person slowing down less than the rest.

Dan Rossum, Broadcaster

[Transcript from TV broadcast]
Fa'atasi's charging hard! He closes the gap! They're tearing toward the finish! Twenty meters to go!

Rebecca Moffet, Color Commentator

[Transcript from TV broadcast]
World-record pace, Dan!

Dan Rossum, Broadcaster
[Transcript from TV broadcast]
Goodness! Falloon and Fa'atasi! Stride for
stride!

Rebecca Moffet, Color Commentator
[Transcript from TV broadcast]
Mirror images!

Dave Falloon, Dad
They were nearing the finish—

Diane Falloon, Mom
And then—

Dave Falloon, Dad
And then—

Leonard Lish, Emmy-Winning TV Producer
I couldn't believe it—

Dave Falloon, Dad
They both *stopped*.

Leonard Lish, Emmy-Winning TV Producer
Imagine a wave washing up on the shore.
It's coming, it's coming, it's coming . . . and

then it just stops *right* before your feet and
hovers there. That was them just before
the finish line. They stood there, chests
heaving, looking around at the crowd.

Jay Fa'atasi, USA
And then—like we'd planned—we sat down,
back-to-back.

Grant Falloon, Grantsylvania
We locked arms.

Jay Fa'atasi, USA
Like, for that moment, we owned that little
piece of the earth.

Grant Falloon, Grantsylvania
No one was going to move us.

Leonard Lish, Emmy-Winning TV Producer
The confetti operator—I guess assuming the
boys were going to finish—he'd accidentally
pushed the button.

Jay Fa'atasi, USA
Yeah. So all this golden confetti was raining
down on us. It was just chaos, man.

Franny Falloon, Brother
Babblemoney was over by the money, vein
bulging in her neck, yelling, "This will not
do! This will not *do*!"

Diane Falloon, Mom
The security guards—the commandos who'd
been protecting the money—they started
running toward the boys like they were
going to drag them away.

Dave Falloon, Dad
But then the coolest thing happened.

Franny Falloon, Brother
If you look back at the footage, you can
see all the other kids lining the track for
the final, ready for what would happen
next.

Devon Jones, Jamaica
We all knew. We raced out and formed a
wall around Grant and Jay.

Dave Falloon, Dad
It was like seeing shields locked together in
an ancient phalanx or something.

Diane Falloon, Mom

But the shields were *phones.*

Dave Falloon, Dad

They were all filming.

Diane Falloon, Mom

The guards wouldn't go near them. They put their hands up and stepped back.

Grant Falloon, Grantsylvania

Franny was ready for his big moment. He'd hacked into the giant HD screen.

Jay Fa'atasi, USA

And there they were—the kids we'd talked to last night—from all around the world—Hilmi and Xu and Sannjh—telling their stories—showing photos of the factories. All of this happening in perfect order, just like we'd planned.

Franny Falloon, Brother

The crowd was stunned at first . . . watching the giant screen . . .

Grant Falloon, Grantsylvania

And then they started booing. Throwing stuff.

Jay Fa'atasi, USA

At that point Babblemoney realized the crowd had turned on her. She was speeding down the track on her scooter, trying to make a getaway. Well, that's not the best way to put it. Her scooter was super slow. [Laughs.]

Franny Falloon, Brother

The scooter was moving so slow, she was like a sitting duck. But somehow everyone kept missing. Finally this hot dog came down and doinked her right in the head. [Laughs.] It was glorious.

Jay Fa'atasi, USA

I'll be honest, as it all went down, I was expecting the cops to just arrest her on the spot—

Grant Falloon, Grantsylvania

Yeah, I was picturing her led off in cuffs, muttering, *And I would've gotten away with it if not for you pesky kids!* [Laughs.]

Jay Fa'atasi, USA

But that didn't happen.

Grant Falloon, Grantsylvania

Nope. Instead . . . I couldn't believe it . . .
they escorted *us* off the property. Like *we*
were the ones who'd broken the rules.

Jay Fa'atasi, USA

Which I guess . . . we had?

Dave Falloon, Dad

[Sighs.] It's hard to explain this to your
kids. How sometimes even when you're
doing what you know in your heart is
right . . .

Diane Falloon, Mom

You can still be punished for it.

Dave Falloon, Dad

In the moment you're not treated like a
hero.

Diane Falloon, Mom

You're treated like a criminal.

Grant Falloon, Grantsylvania

Obviously the hardest part was giving up
the million bucks.

Jay Fa'atasi, USA

Trust me, we *thought* about taking it.

Grant Falloon, Grantsylvania

But we knew we had to fight back in a different way.

Franny Falloon, Brother

People like Babblemoney . . . the only way to hurt them is to go after their *image*. That's what's propping up their whole empires.

Grant Falloon, Grantsylvania

We realized we could make Babblemoney pay in more ways than one.

Adriana Santos, Brazil

After Grant and Jay told us what was really going on, the girls made a pact that whoever won would give the money to the families who had been hurt in the factories.

Maggie Olinyk, Ukraine

That was hard. I mean, it's not like my family is rich. We could have really used that money.

Adriana Santos, Brazil

But everyone agreed. Which made it easier.

Maggie Olinyk, Ukraine

Maybe this isn't the kind of thing I should admit . . . but I was also imagining how many likes and retweets we would all get from doing the right thing . . . everyone cheering us on in the comments. . . . I know, it's so messed up, but I'd be lying if I said I didn't think about that.

Franny Falloon, Brother

It's easy to think that a "good" person always acts for the right reasons, and a "bad" person always acts for the wrong reasons. But I think it's more complicated. Like, I think we did the right thing. I'm proud of what we did. But—let's be honest—my ego was still a big part of wanting to do this. I wanted the praise! Of course I did. Though it was a little easier for me because I wasn't out there racing.

Grant Falloon, Grantsylvania

It's easy to look back now and say we made the right choice. But it's much harder in the moment. My biggest fear was that we were going to execute this whole plan perfectly . . . and it wasn't going to matter. We'd just get crushed like little bugs and everyone would laugh at us and the world would keep right on spinning. We talked about that a lot the night before. Is this even worth it? Is this our fight?

Jay Fa'atasi, USA

But then we just kept coming back to the people. Real people were getting hurt. We'd talked to their kids. We'd seen their faces. It's like—imagine if it was happening right in front of you. You see someone getting hurt. You see the look on their face, the pain. Of course you'd try to help that person. But somehow it's different when it's far away. You can block it out and just go on with your life. Does that make you a bad person? Not necessarily. [Thinks.] Or does it? We just had to keep reminding ourselves what really mattered. Who we wanted to stand with.

Grant Falloon, Grantsylvania

So yeah. The boys made a pact too. We

said that whoever made the final would do the protest. So that way the girls would take Babblemoney's million, get it in the bank, and then we would come next and blow the lid off the whole thing.

Jay Fa'atasi, USA
But we weren't done with Babblemoney just yet. That night Franny slowed down the video of her getting hit with the hot dog. We watched it wobble toward her head, frame by frame, laughing so hard. He put it online, and overnight she became the most famous meme of the year—even bigger than Grant tripping at the Penn Relays. The way Egyptian royalty got mummified? Yeah. She got *meme*-ified. [Laughs.]

Grant Falloon, Grantsylvania
Plus, because our release forms were forged, they weren't allowed to use our images in their commercials. They had nothing.

Diane Falloon, Mom
[Neck turning red.] It all worked out. But let's not get in the habit. . . .

Grant Falloon, Grantsylvania

And actually, other sneaker companies have reached out to us since then, offering us sponsorships. We're still weighing our options. . . .

Jay Fa'atasi, USA

It's kind of crazy if you think about it. If Grant hadn't been raised the way he was, and if I hadn't moved to East Falls in fourth grade, and if he hadn't tripped at the Penn Relays, and a zillion other things, all in just the right order . . . none of this would've happened. Turns out this was our destiny all along. We just couldn't see it.

Grant Falloon, Grantsylvania

Or maybe we've got the whole idea of destiny wrong. Maybe our destiny isn't written in advance like a script. Maybe our destiny is actually changing all the time, as we change, new lanes opening up before us as others fade.

Jay Fa'atasi, USA

[Nodding.] Whoa. That's deep, bro. I like that.

Grant Falloon, Grantsylvania

I don't know if it's true. But it reminds me that my choices matter, you know? It's all happening live, right in front of us, and we get to decide what happens.

Jay Fa'atasi, USA

So what's gonna happen next, Mr. Smart Guy?

Grant Falloon, Grantsylvania

[Laughs.] You'll have to subscribe to find out.

37

Before we flew home from California, me, Mom, Dad, Franny, Mrs. Fa'atasi, Tua, and Jay all rented bikes and went out for a long ride. It was funny—we were like a *super*-peloton, all of us in matching helmets and reflective vests.

"Pothole!" Mom yelled, and we all swerved around it.

We rode through the mountains, enjoying the scenery, and soon enough we saw it—the faded sign that said WELCOME TO THE GOLDEN STATE FAMILY COMMUNE: WHERE FRIENDS ARE FAMILY!

Except when we turned up the driveway . . . it was gone. All that was left was a broken-down school bus propped on cinder blocks.

"We lived right over there," Dad said, pointing to a cluster of falling-down shacks. I closed my eyes, and it was like I traveled through time. I saw Young Mom, in a long flowered dress, and Young Dad, in a baggy flannel shirt, showing up on their first day, nervous but excited to build a new kind of family. I saw them sitting around a campfire, laughing, Mom palming her pregnant belly. I saw them packing up their clothes years later, feeling like they'd failed, but doing what they needed to do for their kids.

And when I opened my eyes—and I saw us all there together, the Falloons and the Fa'atasis, it felt like—through me—their dream had been realized. The baton had been passed. We all squeezed in for a selfie in front of the broken-down school bus, and I thought, *This is my family, all of us, no matter what the paperwork says.*

Two weeks later, I'm back in East Falls. School starts again tomorrow, my first lap on a brand-new track—*high school*. I've been having these nightmares where I'm lost in a locker-lined maze and I can never find the right classroom.

"You'll be fine," Dad says, drawing in his sketchpad at the kitchen table. "You just have to show up, put your feet in the starting rocks, and—"

"They're called starting *blocks*, Dad."

"Well whatever. You get my point."

He holds up the sketchbook and shows me the idea for his new Dracula doll. "Modern Dracula" wears a cool band T-shirt (the Impalers) and skinny jeans, and demands to know where all his blood is sourced from.

I have to laugh. "You're so weird, Dad."

"Yeah? And that's a bad thing?"

Mom's still waking up at four a.m. to review her case files. It's hard work, but she knows that if she doesn't do it, no one will.

And it's worth it: A few weeks ago she noticed a conflicting timeline in a police report and saved an innocent man from spending the rest of his life in jail. The man's kids sent us handmade thank-you letters, colorful stick figures with their arms all joined together. They're hanging on the fridge now.

As of last week, Franny has officially taken over the Grantsylvania channel. He's been driving me nuts, begging me to guest-star all the time ("The people demand it!"), but at least I know his heart is in the right place. He really believes this "life-streaming" is the wave of the future. He says it's great because we can "open our borders" and, at the same time, travel and see the world from lots of different points of view. He says it's how we'll connect and make the world a better place.

Maybe someday we'll come to think of this "life-streaming" like books, how you can transport into another consciousness for a while to enrich your own.

It's hard to imagine, but Franny has always been able to see multiple steps ahead—he's fast like that. Who knows, maybe one day he really will win that Nobel Prize—or at least an Emmy.

I'm on the fenced-in bridge over the highway, just after dawn. I still plan to break Usain Bolt's record someday, and it's not gonna just magically happen. I have to work for it. I have to train every day. It's a Sunday morning, so there's no traffic right now, just an occasional car flashing by like a comet.

"Bro," Jay says, appearing from his side of the bridge. "What's the deal?"

"What are you talking about?"

"Didn't you get my text?"

"Nah. I left my phone. What's up?"

"Dude, it's hilarious. Check it out."

He takes out his phone and shows me the site he made last night. It's a picture of us with our arms locked in protest at the Million Dollar Race. Above us, a digital clock is counting up infinitely.

"We never finished," Jay says, "so technically the clock is still running. Every day it just keeps adding up and up. So if you think about it, we actually *did* break the world record. Both of us."

"We did?"

"Yeah, man. We ran the *slowest* hundred-meter dash of all time!"

I laugh and punch him in the arm. I worried for a long time that we couldn't be best friends *and* rivals. That the DNA of our friendship was flawed.

But now I see that that's dumb. We're best friends *because* we compete. We push each other. We make each other better every day.

"Race you to the end of the bridge," he says. "Winner gets the last slice at Franks."

I smirk. "You're on."

For us, anything can be a finish line. A house. A tree. A telephone pole. A stray cat. It never ends.

We bend our knees, side by side.

Ready . . .

Set . . .

Go!

I take off, arms pumping, the biggest smile on my face. When I'm running, it's like time moves differently. I can feel myself passing through the seconds like they're a physical place.

I drive with my legs, exploding forward with maximum force. I go faster and faster, becoming blurrier and blurrier, until I'm no longer the kid dodging stares at school. I'm no longer the kid who re-writes his social media posts ten times, worried what people will think. I'm just a beam of light hurtling through time and space.

That's the hardest part to explain to non-runners. Yes, the point is to reach the finish line. Yes, you're charging toward it with everything you've got—back straight, elbows in, fingers fully extended.

Eyes. On. The. Prize.

But at the same time, deep down, a part of you *doesn't* want to get there. You wish the finish line would just keep receding so you could stay inside this moment, and this feeling, forever.

THE END

ACKNOWLEDGMENTS

A huge thanks to my editors, Anna Parsons and Alyson Heller. This book changed a lot, over many years, and I'm so lucky to have had your insight and support. Thanks to my agent, Melissa Edwards, for your relentless advocacy of my work. Thanks to the world-class team at Aladdin books—Heather Palisi, Elizabeth Mims, Sara Berko, and Mara Anastas—as well as cover illustrator Oriol Vidal. Thanks to Fiona Simpson for your support when this was just a weird little seed of an idea. Thanks to Jason Finau for schooling me on Samoan-American family life. Thanks to all the hardworking teachers and librarians out there getting books like this into the hands of young readers. I'm so grateful for the work you do. Thanks to my son, Quentin, who is reading this in the distant land of the future: hi! And thanks, most of all, to Georgia: I got grief for putting you at the bottom last time, but sorry, that's where the most important person goes. I love ya.

ABOUT THE AUTHOR

A brief conversation with Matthew Ross Smith

Q: *The Million Dollar Race* **combines a traditional first-person narrative with an oral history format. Why did you choose to tell the story that way?**

A: Well, a novel about a sprinter has to move fast. Switching between the formats keeps the story racing forward. Also, I think the oral history sections mirror the way we consume sports and reality TV. I always think it's cool when a novel's structure is shaped by its subject matter. I even briefly considered selling sponsorships (Chapter One, presented by Frank's Pizza!). That would've been funny.

Q: How long does it take you to write a novel?

A: I usually bang it out in a week or two, then go back and do a quick read-through for typos.

Q: Is that true?

A: No. It takes years. I'm lucky to have a really smart team backing me up. Sometimes you need someone to peel you off the track, point you in the right direction, and say, "You got this. Keep going."

Q: So I guess you wanted to be an author when you were a kid?

A: No! I never wrote anything when I was a kid!

Q: Come on. *Nothing?*

A: Well, just the boring stuff I had to write for school. In sixth grade I wrote an essay about my cousin, Luke, who had died. I didn't think about it too much. I just wrote what I felt, and I handed it in. Next day the teacher, Mr. Batt, made me read it aloud in front of the whole class. Afterward there was this stunned silence in the room. I mean, in a *good* way. I liked that.

In high school I started writing silly things for the school paper. The goal was to make my friends laugh. That was all I cared about. I remember seeing my mom reading one of my articles in the living room one night, laughing *so* hard, and that made me feel good.

But it was still a while after that before I started to take writing seriously. So if you're out there and you already want to be a writer—awesome. You're ahead of the game. If you're out there farting around like I was—that's cool too. You've got time.

Q: How does an author decide what to name their characters?

A: For me, it's musical. You play the note. It sounds right or it doesn't. That's usually it. But in this case I was also thinking about one of my favorite writers, Kurt Vonnegut. He has this concept of a *granfalloon* that I think relates to the book in an interesting way. It's not worth explaining in detail here, but you can google it if you want. I hide lots of Easter eggs like that in my books, mostly for myself.

Q: What are some other ones?

A: Well I'm not gonna just *tell* you. . . .

Q: If you could have your readers take one lesson away from this book, what would it be?

A: Hmm. That's a tough one. I don't write books to teach life lessons. They're like a pleasant, unintended side effect. They happen if I do my job well.

But since you asked, if readers take only one thing from *The Million Dollar Race*, I hope it's the Falloons' family motto—"Skepsis!" Question everything! In these surreal times critical thinking is more important than ever. For real.